EAGLE'S PREY

Sheriff Ike Hardy was on the trail of a pair of vicious killers who had robbed a stage and shot the two passengers. The trouble was that Ike was no tracker, but when he encountered a buckskin-clad mountaineer who could trail anyone or anything, he thought he had a good chance of catching the killers. However, he had been led into a trap and the killers were bent on adding a kidnap to their list of crimes. It was going to be a long and bloody struggle before Colt justice was done.

BILLY HALL

EAGLE'S PREY

Complete and Unabridged

LINFORD
Leicester

First published in Great Britain in 2003 by
Robert Hale Limited
London

First Linford Edition
published 2004
by arrangement with
Robert Hale Limited
London

The moral right of the author
has been asserted

British Library CIP Data

Hall, Billy
  Eagle's prey.—Large print ed.—
Linford western library
  1. Western stories
  2. Large type books
  I. Title
  823.9'14 [F]

  ISBN 1–84395–456–7

Published by
F. A. Thorpe (Publishing)
Anstey, Leicestershire

Set by Words & Graphics Ltd.
Anstey, Leicestershire
Printed and bound in Great Britain by
T. J. International Ltd., Padstow, Cornwall

This book is printed on acid-free paper

1

The eagle's scream drifted on the breeze. It echoed from the mountain cliffs, and faded into the limitless expanse of blue sky. Coralee Sternhagen shielded her eyes from the bright sun, trying to catch a glimpse of the great bird.

Small white clouds drifted lazily against the deep blue background of the Wyoming sky. Tall pines and spruce made a varied pattern that almost seemed deliberate, as their different shades of green blended into each other. In places, the lighter shade of aspen trees altered the motif, giving it life. That life took movement and form as a playful breeze toyed with the leaves, giving the groves the illusion of giggling and trembling at the mirth of the frivolous breeze.

Beneath the trees, June grass brimmed

with life and vigor, striving upward toward the sun. Its verdant carpet promised food for cattle and wildlife alike, pleading to be eaten that its life might be shared and dispersed.

The horse, with her reins hanging loose to the ground, was doing her best to co-operate. Her teeth tore loose a tall clump of grass with an audible rip. Coralee, or Corky as she was known to everyone, turned her attention momentarily back from the sky at the noise. Smiling at the long stems of grass sticking out of both sides of her horse's mouth, she resumed looking for the eagle.

Behind her the tall peaks of the mountain range loomed. Deeply snow-covered at this early month, their brilliant white points stretched up in a never-ending effort to touch the clouds.

The eagle screamed again, and Corky spotted its immense wingspan. As she watched, it folded its wings and dived toward a towering spruce tree. It struck the tree fifteen or twenty feet below its top, then veered away. Its massive wings beat in mighty strokes, dodging the tops of other trees as it fought to regain altitude.

Right behind it, another eagle of equal size dived at the same tree. It veered just before striking the tree, and circled upward. It screamed again, its voice sounding angry and frustrated.

Corky frowned. She picked up the reins of her horse, and rode toward a ridge that would give her a better view of the tree. It would also change the direction of her gaze, so the sun would not be so much in her eyes.

Achieving the top of the ridge, she dismounted again. From one of her saddle-bags she removed a large pair of binoculars. Directing them toward the giant tree, she fiddled with the adjustments until it came into sharp focus. Then she began following the huge trunk upward. As she reached the top branches of the tree, she spotted a large nest of twigs and branches. Just as she centered the binoculars on it, one of the eagles landed in the nest. It shifted around the nest, scolding in a raspy, scratchy voice, then settling out of sight.

'I never heard an eagle do that before,' Corky marveled. 'I've only heard their screaming. Maybe I've just never been this close to one that was upset before. I wonder what she's mad at?'

No sooner had she said it than the eagle emerged into view at the side of the nest. It looked groundward, craning its neck, scolding, then giving a more typically eagle-like scream.

Moving the glasses downward, Corky caught movement in the tree. Searching carefully, she soon spotted two gray squirrels. Amongst the branches of the tree, they flitted and scurried. She could faintly make out their chattering. One or the other constantly scuttled upward toward the edges of the nest, immediately driven back by the head of the eagle reaching over the side.

Corky gasped in sudden understanding. 'They're trying to get at her eggs! They're going to try to eat them before they hatch! No wonder she's mad. And she can't get at them, because the squirrels stay among the branches where the eagles can't reach them.'

As she watched, the other eagle swooped down again, trying to pluck a squirrel from the side of the tree. Once again he was frustrated by those branches. The squirrels seemed to take great delight in the whole game. They chattered and skittered about busily, their tails bobbing and curling constantly.

Corky reached out and touched the stock of the rifle extending from her saddle scabbard. Her brow furrowed. She sighed deeply.

'There's no way I could come close to those squirrels from here,' she muttered. 'And if I get closer, the branches will keep me from getting a clear shot. That tree's got to be over a hundred feet high. I wonder why the eagles built a nest there? I thought they always put it up on the side of a cliff somewhere.'

As she puzzled the situation, she trained her glasses back on the tree once more. Just as she spotted the squirrels again, a black-and-white blur passed by the lens. She jumped and squealed softly. She giggled. 'That scared me! What was it?'

Less than thirty seconds after she refocused the binoculars it happened again. 'Magpie,' she breathed. 'There's another one. And another. What are they doing? Oh, look! They're going after the squirrels!'

As she watched, entranced, a flock of magpies wove among the branches of the giant tree, screeching and pecking at the pair of squirrels. For a while, the squirrels made a game of it, dodging from side to side of the tree, up and down, branch to branch. Every time they dodged to the other side of the tree, however, there were more magpies coming at them from that side. They soon abandoned the tree, leaping from branch to branch, scrambling lower into the thicker foliage of the forest. Their flight and the heavier parts of the forest thwarted the magpies' attack, and the flock of the black-and-white birds flew away.

Lifting her glasses back to the aerie at the top of the tree, Corky was just in time to see the second eagle return. In its great talons it held the limp body of a cottontail rabbit. As though the incident with the squirrels was already a dim and forgotten memory, the two began tearing at the warm flesh of the shared meal.

She sighed again, and returned the binoculars to the saddle-bag. 'I never saw anything like that!' Corky said softly.

She swung easily into the saddle. 'Come on, Belle,' she told her horse. 'We better head for home. Besides, I want to ask Papa if he's ever seen anything like that before.'

2

'Oh, Papa, you should have seen it!' Corky exulted. 'The squirrels were trying their best to get at the eggs, and the eagles — both of them — it was a pair — and they were swooping and diving and screaming. I've never seen anything like it!'

Ira Sternhagen's blue eyes twinkled. His pride in his daughter was a palpable thing as he listened to her enthuse. His voice, however, was slow and thoughtful.

'Whoa up a mite there, Little Filly,' he drawled. 'What're you talkin' about?'

Corky shook her long blonde hair back from her face. Her eyes mirrored her father's twinkle, as they danced and glistened. 'It was eagles, Papa. I was riding up along the Thompson Rim. It's so pretty up there. It's always quiet, and the grass is so deep and green. Anyway,

I kept hearing eagles screaming, more than they do just hunting, and I looked and looked before I found them. They'd built a nest clear up in the top of a really big old spruce tree. Do they do that often?'

Ira fussed with his pipe, holding a twig from the fireplace to the bowl and drawing on it, until the tobacco lit and a great cloud of smoke encircled his head. He shook his head.

'Not often,' he replied. 'Most o' the time they like to find a ledge o' rock along some high cliff, where varmints an' such can't get to it. That way they can leave the nest to hunt when the sun's warm. They only usually sit on their eggs of a night, or when it's cold and rainy. When the sun shines, it keeps 'em plenty warm. Built it in a tree, you say?'

Corky nodded. 'Clear up at the very top, but in the tree, yes. And a couple squirrels were trying their best to get at the nest. Will squirrels eat eggs, Papa?'

Ira exhaled a cloud of smoke and

nodded again. 'Sure. They're pretty much a bushy-tailed rat what lives in trees. They'll eat most anything. They'll chew a hole in the end of an egg and eat everything that runs out.'

'Well, that must have been what they were trying to do, then. Every time the mother eagle would leave the nest, they'd try to climb in it. Then she'd swoop down, screaming and diving, and the squirrels would run down the tree a ways. Then the eagle would wait a while and leave, and they'd try again. Then the other eagle came. I think it must have been her mate. And they both started trying to get at the squirrels, but they couldn't, because the squirrels would run down the tree far enough so the branches would protect them. The eagles would swoop in and tear off branches with a big crash, and try to bust their way to where the squirrels were, but they could never reach them.'

'I 'spect the squirrels was havin' some fun out of it,' Ira suggested.

'They acted it,' she agreed. 'They'd

chatter and scold like everything. I found a spot high enough so that I could see over most of the trees, and close enough to even hear the squirrels.'

'You musta been on that big yeller ridge that juts out just above the spring.'

'Yes! I thought you'd know the place. Anyway, I guess the eagles must have a way to talk with other birds.'

Ira puffed his pipe thoughtfully, frowning through the smoke. 'What makes you say that?'

'Well, after it had gone on for quite a while, and eagles were screaming and diving into the trees, and the squirrels were chattering and scampering around, a whole flock of magpies came along.'

'Nasty bird!' Ira huffed. 'I sure hate 'em. They'll commence to pickin' on a calf, after he's been branded, or if he's got a sore, and they'll swarm around him and pick at the raw place, makin' it bigger'n bigger, till they eat enough of 'im to kill 'im. Then they'll just go off

11

an' leave 'im, an' let the coyotes and buzzards eat the rest of 'im. They're worse'n buzzards. Don't even wait for nothin' to die, afore they start in. Filthy, nasty birds.'

Corky ignored the outburst. 'But these were after the squirrels. They swarmed around the tree, and no matter what side of the tree the squirrels went on, there were magpies there, flying around and darting in and pecking at them. One of them knocked one of the squirrels clear off the tree, and he fell about five or six feet before he grabbed onto another branch. They kept it up until they drove the squirrels clear out of that tree and chased them away. I guess they were coming to the rescue of the eagles.'

Ira shook his head. 'No such thing, Little Filly,' he disagreed. 'Birds cain't talk to one another. They can make lots o' noises, and most animals know what a lot o' the noises mean, but they don't really talk. Not like folks. I 'spect the magpies was attracted by all the commotion. That much commotion usually means a scrap o' some kind, and any kinda scrap means somethin's likely to get left dead. They was just lookin' for an easy meal. Once they got there, though, they seen them squirrels. Squirrels is as much a natural enemy o' magpies as any other bird. More'n the eagles, even, 'cause they always nest in trees, an' have to fight the squirrels. So they just naturally took after the squirrels an' tried to kill 'em.'

'Are you sure?'

'Of course. Aesop an' a host of other fellas have written stories an' books an' such, that make animals out to be sorta four-legged people that have a language we can't understand. They do that just to make a point that folks wouldn't likely understand if they just told 'em straight out. Like *Androcles an' the Lion*, fer instance. You remember me readin' that one to you? You could tell folks to be kind to one another, an' that kindness'll come back to you, sooner or later, but it wouldn't have the same way o' sneakin' into people's hearts an' changing 'em. Truth is, though, animals is just animals. They don't think about who they are, or why they're here, or what's gonna happen tomorrow. They just do what the good lord designed 'em to do, 'cause they got no choice. It's just in 'em.'

Corky sighed heavily. 'I suppose. But it really looked like the eagles sent out some sort of message to the cavalry, and the whole troop of cavalry came flying in and rescued them.'

Ira chuckled. He started to reply, but his mother chose that moment to wander into the room. Her body was bony and frail. Her cheekbones appeared almost to jut through the transparent skin, mottled here and there with age spots. Her eyes were distant, but her voice was strong.

In a flat voice, but one that trembled with emotion she said, 'Oh, I am so ashamed. I never thought I would get caught, that way. I never should have done such a thing. Oh, my parents are going to be so disappointed in me. They are going to be so hurt. I have such wonderful parents. They have always been so proud of me. They are going to be so ashamed and so hurt. My daddy will come and get me. He will get me out of here. But he is going to be so hurt. I don't want to see my daddy cry. I don't know why I ever even thought of doing such a thing. I don't want to be here. I want to go home. They won't let me leave. But my parents will come and get me. My mother will be so ashamed. She was always so proud of me. I don't want my parents to even know about it. But I have to tell them. They have to find out. I can't get out of here if they don't come and get me. Oh, I am so ashamed.'

As she rambled on, she shuffled on through the room and out the other side. She appeared not to see either one of them. Ira sighed heavily.

Corky frowned. 'Whatever is she talking about, Papa? Did Mamaw do something bad once? She talks like she's in jail or something.'

Ira shook his head. He reached into the edge of the fireplace and tapped his pipe, knocking the ashes into the fire.

'Why do we have a fire going, anyway?' Corky asked, before he could answer her first question.

Ira chose to answer the last question first. 'Ma was cold. Thought it wouldn't hurt to light a fire for a little bit.'

'She's always cold,' Corky observed.

Ira nodded in agreement. 'Old folks mostly is.'

'Do you know what she did?' Corky insisted.

Ira shook his head again. 'Don't have any idea. As far as I ever knew, she never did a thing wrong in her whole life. I 'spect she must've, though. Now she's gone feeble-minded, an' can't remember much of anything. I ain't even sure she knows who we are any more. She can't remember anything, 'cept that one thing, whatever it was. I 'spect maybe it happened, all right. I

16

'spect it was the worst thing she ever did, an' she got caught, an' her pa had to come an' get her. Mighta just been swipin' a pickle outa the barrel at the store or somethin'. She won't never tell us what she's talkin' about. Her mind's just stuck on that one thing. The worst day of her life, likely, an' now she's stuck with livin' it over an' over an' over.'

'That is so sad.'

Ira sighed again. 'It is, for a fact.'

'I don't even remember you going back to bring her out here to live with us.'

'I didn't.'

Corky's eyebrows shot up. 'You didn't? How did she get here, then?'

'She just showed up,' Ira explained. 'I 'spect you must've been, oh, maybe four. We still lived in the old house. The one Bull and Sadie have. She just showed up. Come into the yard ridin' in a buggy she'd hired at the livery barn, clear down at Cheyenne. Rode the train out that far. Said Pa'd died, so she'd sold the place and come out here to live with us.'

'Were you glad?'

Ira rose from his chair. 'I 'spect supper's about ready.' He avoided the question.

Frowning, Corky followed him and the smell of roast beef to the kitchen.

3

'And just what is the prettiest lady in Fremont County doing sitting there on the ground? Did your horse throw you?'

Corky looked up into the wide grin of Arn Banning. His bright-blue eyes flashed merriment. He sat his horse in a way that almost made it look as if he were strutting, but he seemed unconscious of the fact. She wondered at the feelings that tingled through her, looking at him. She smiled at him.

'Hello, Arn. No, I'm fine. My horse is right over there. I was just watching the geese.'

'Those are big geese,' he agreed. 'Canadas.'

'Canadas?'

He nodded, stepping down from his horse. He sat on the ground, almost against her. 'Canada geese.'

'I don't think these are. They nest right here, every summer. I can remember several years ago, when I first started watching them, there was just the one pair. They had five baby geese, and they went south for the winter. Then, in the spring, when they came back, three of the young ones came back too, only now they all had a mate. There were four nests, then. The three young pairs, and the old pair. I guess some of them must get shot or killed or something every year, or else there'd be more of them than the lake could support by now. But there must be twenty-five or more now. But they all nest here. They aren't Canada geese at all.'

'That's just what they're called,' he explained. 'There's different kinds of geese. Canada geese, like these, are the biggest. The white ones are snow geese. I don't know what the others are, but there's lots o' kinds o' geese. All good eatin'.'

She nodded. 'Papa gets out his

shotgun and shoots three or four every year,' she said.

'How's he get close enough?'

'He uses old Nellie.'

'The old work-horse?'

Corky nodded. 'He puts a halter on her, and walks her out along the water, when the geese are close. Or if they're in that field of oats, he leads her out there. He walks beside her, on the opposite side from the geese. He walks right by her front legs, so the geese can't see his legs under the horse's belly. Then when he gets up close, he sticks the shotgun under Nellie's neck and shoots.'

'Don't that spook the horse?'

Corky giggled. 'Oh, sure. Nellie snorts and her head and her tail shoot up in the air, and she takes off in that big old clumsy gallop of hers, and sometimes she kicks with both hind legs, and she runs clear back to the barn. But, by the next day, she's forgot all about it, and Papa leads her out to get another goose.'

Arn chuckled. 'Looks like she'd wise up and not be so willin', when your pa's carryin' the gun.'

Corky nodded. 'It looks like it, but she never does. I think she's figured out it's a game, and she never gets hurt, so she just plays the game. Papa doesn't even have to tell her where to stop any more. She just walks out to the closest they can get to the geese, and waits for Papa to shoot, then she throws her tail up and runs.'

'Even animals like to have their fun, huh?' Arn suggested.

'Sure. Don't you?'

His eyes darted up and down over her body before he answered. She felt her face turn crimson at the unspoken response to her question, but his words did not press the issue.

'Of course,' he said easily. 'That's what life is for. If we can't have a little fun once in a while, life'd get pretty hard.'

'What do you do for fun?' she asked him unexpectedly.

His eyes darted over her body again. In spite of her embarrassment, she had to admit she liked the feelings that surged in her when he looked at her like that. 'Oh, same's most cowpokes,' he evaded. 'Go off to town an' spend my wages.'

'Do you have a, I mean, are you, uh, courting someone?'

'Naw! I had a girl down in Cheyenne, though. She was pertneart as pretty as you are.'

The glow of the returning blush made her feel warm all over. 'Why did you leave there?'

His eyes clouded, but his expression didn't change otherwise. 'She had a couple brothers that thought my intentions weren't honorable. They made things sorta hot for me. I decided no girl was worth gettin' killed over. I rode off up here an' went to work for your pa.'

'And were your intentions honorable?'

His eyes danced. 'As honorable as

she wanted 'em to be.'

'Do you miss her?'

He nodded. 'Somethin' fierce. She was a fine, fine woman. She could make me feel things I didn't think anyone could feel.'

'What do you mean?'

His eyes darted the length of her body again, pausing a brief moment on the front of her blouse.

'Just could,' he evaded. 'Takes a fine woman to not be afraid to love a man.'

Corky was suddenly uncomfortable with the direction of the conversation, but she wasn't sure why. She turned her attention back to the geese.

'Oh, look,' she said, 'she's going to leave the nest. I didn't think they ever left the nest till the other one got there to watch the eggs.'

Arn's surprise was apparent. 'They take turns?' he asked.

Corky nodded a little too vigorously, glad to have a direction to turn the conversation. 'Oh, yes. Geese mate for life, you know. They're not like ducks. If a goose gets killed, the other one will keep coming back for weeks, looking for its mate. That's why Papa always tries to shoot both geese of the same pair when he shoots them, so he won't leave one to grieve the other.'

'They don't never mate up again?' Arn asked.

'Oh, yes. The next spring they will. But not until then. And they take turns sitting on the eggs to keep them warm, and to keep animals from eating them or something.'

'That so? Don't look like that one remembered what he was supposed to do.'

'That's the male,' she said. 'You can tell because he's a little bigger than the female. He must be hungry, and he's not waiting for her to get back. He's just flying away. Oh, I hope the eggs will be OK.'

'Not for long,' Arn said, pointing.

She followed the direction of his

point. She gasped with a sharp intake of her breath. 'Ravens! They must have been just sitting there watching the nest. They're flying right toward it.'

'Yup,' Arn agreed. A smile played at the corners of his mouth. 'They're about to have one fine dinner.'

The ravens landed on the edge of the nest, looking around busily. Then one of them hopped into the center of the nest and immediately began pecking at one of the eggs. Corky's hands flew to her mouth.

'Oh, Arn. Stop them! They're eating the eggs! There are probably baby geese in the eggs already. They'll kill them!'

''Course they will,' Arn agreed. 'They ain't gonna pass up that good a meal, just sittin' there waitin' for 'em.'

'So stop them!'

'Why?'

'Because they'll kill the baby geese!'

Arn shrugged. 'That's the way of life, pretty lady. Everything that lives,

lives off the life of something else. Everything that dies provides life for something that doesn't. Nature balances things out that way. It's best not to interfere.'

Corky leaped to her feet. Her eyes darted back and forth between him and the goose nest. Four ravens were busily pecking away at the unseen contents of the nest.

'Give me your gun. I'll scare them away.'

'I don't never hand my gun to anybody,' Arn said very softly. 'Not even to a beautiful lady. But if I was ever to do that, I guess you'd be the one that could make me do it.'

She was suddenly aware of a whole new sense of his presence. He had stood when she did. He stood now, almost against her. He was a good half a head taller than she, and she felt as if he were towering over her. She wanted to move away from him, but at the same time wanted to move against him, to snuggle against his side.

'I — I think I should be going,' she mumbled.

Arn put an arm around her waist, holding her there, pulling her slightly closer to him. He pointed with his other hand.

'Look,' he said. 'Your eggs are about to get rescued.'

Her attention torn between the arm around her waist and the nest of eggs, she looked up. A goose was flying toward the nest, flying low and fast. The ravens spotted it at the same time. One of them squawked loudly, and took off in a flurry of wings. The rest followed suit immediately, pursued at once by the goose.

The goose was faster than the ravens, but they were a great deal more maneuverable in the air. They twisted and dodged, flying off in different directions. The goose pursued one of them for a ways, then wheeled and flew back to the nest. She landed on the edge of the nest, surveying the remains of broken eggs, strewn about the nest.

Only a small portion of each gosling had been eaten, but none would survive.

'Oh, look at the poor thing!' Corky empathized. 'Oh, she looks so forlorn, sitting there. What must that feel like?'

She was only vaguely aware that Arn had removed his hat and dropped it on the ground. He moved around in front of her, as if to shield her from the distressing sight. He put his arms around her, pulling her against him. She allowed herself to be pressed against him, glad for the strength of his manliness, the comforting smell of his presence.

Other feelings began to well up within her. For a moment they felt heady, exciting, demanding. Then they suddenly became alarming. She pushed abruptly away from him.

'I better head back to the house,' she said, brushing at the front of her blouse.

Arn smiled. 'What's your hurry? I like your company. When I'm close to

29

you I can forget everything else in the world.'

Corky tried to ignore the crimson heat of her face. 'I — I like being with you, too, Arn, but I — I've got to go.'

She hurried to her horse. She grabbed the saddle horn and leaped into the saddle without touching the stirrups. Then she paused and smiled impudently down at Arn.

'Better get to work, cowboy. I'll tell Papa you're lolli-gaggin' on the job!'

Without waiting for his answer, she kicked her horse and loped toward the ranch.

She rode into the yard, breathless and flushed. As she dismounted, a young cowboy approached her.

'Want me to take care o' your horse, Miss Corky?'

She smiled brightly at him. 'Oh, would you, Puke? That's awfully sweet of you.'

'My pleasure, ma'am.'

As he started away, she stopped and called out to him. 'That isn't really your name, is it? Puke, I mean.'

He grinned at her. 'No, ma'am. I just sorta got a upset stomach a lot. If'n somethin' don't agree with me, it don't stay down too good. The boys just sorta started callin' me that, an' pretty soon it got to be my name.'

'So what is your name, really?'

'Sean. It's Sean Granger.'

'Well then, I think I'll call you Sean. I like that a lot better than Puke.'

His grin widened. 'Me too. Thanks, ma'am.'

'That is, if you'll call me Corky, instead of ma'am,' she insisted. 'My mother is 'ma'am'.'

'Yes, ma'am. I mean yes, Corky. I'll do that, Corky. I sure will.'

'Thank you for taking care of my horse, Sean.'

'My pleasure, M . . . Corky,' he enthused as he walked away on an invisible cloud.

Corky burst into the house, happy to find her father there.

'Papa, do geese have emotions?'

'What?'

'Do geese feel things. Like happiness and joy and grief and love and things like that?'

'I don't rightly know,' Ira admitted. 'Why?'

'Oh, we . . . I was just watching some geese up at the lake. They both left the nest at the same time. As soon as they were gone, ravens came and pecked open the eggs and ate all the baby geese . . . '

'Goslings,' Ira corrected.

'Goslings,' she accepted, ' . . . and then the goose came back and chased them away, and then just sat there on the edge of the nest looking at what was left in the nest. Her dead babies, I suppose, or what was left of them. I just wondered if she felt grief, or what.'

Ira sighed. 'Hard to say. Probably. Geese are sort of special. They mate for life, you know.'

'I know. You told me.'

'If one of a pair gets killed, the other

one sure seems to grieve for a while, so I 'spect they do. Probably don't remember a long time, though, not like people.'

'Did you and Mama ever lose a baby?'

Ira's eyes clouded. 'Yeah. We lost one. Little boy. Woulda been your little brother. You was nigh on to three. Pertneart lost your ma, too.'

'I didn't know.'

'We don't talk much about it.'

'Why not?'

'Hurts too much.'

'Still?'

'Yeah. It doesn't stop hurting. The hurt sort of settles down into a dull pain that's just there in the back of your mind all the time, and you get used to it, but it's always there.'

'Oh, I am so ashamed,' Ira's mother said as she shuffled into the room. 'I don't know why I ever did anything like that. Oh, my daddy is going to be so hurt. He's going to be so ashamed. He's going to come and get me out of here, but he's going to be so hurt. I wish he didn't have to ever know I did anything like that.'

Her monologue of remorse continued unabated as she wandered through the room and out again.

As she left the room, Ira said, 'I sure hope when I get old I don't get stuck rememberin' something that hurts like that.'

'Or babies dying, or baby geese being eaten out of their eggs,' Corky agreed.

'Goslings,' Ira corrected again.

Silence hung heavily for half a minute. Then Corky said, 'Papa, what does it feel like to be in love?'

Ira frowned. 'What brought that up?'

'Just wondering. Does it feel all tingly and funny?'

'Sometimes,' Ira agreed. 'But you watch them tingly and funny feelings. Sometimes they come just from bein' in heat, not in love.'

Corky giggled. 'Papa!'

As she walked to her room to change

from her riding-clothes, she wondered how many other things about her parents she didn't know. Then she wondered if she would ever know, or if she really wanted to.

4

'They turned south, just over the mountain.'

The words caught Sheriff Ike Hardy by surprise. He jumped violently. He left the saddle in a long dive to the ground. Landing on his shoulder, he rolled to his right, sprang to his feet and dove behind a wild-plum thicket.

He came to his feet in a crouch, gun in hand.

The voice laughed. 'Now that's a right smart set o' moves, it is. 'Course, if'n I was aimin' to shoot ya, you'd a been dead a'ready afore you started 'em.'

Ike moved soundlessly backward, looking around for an avenue to circle the bodiless voice. He had taken three steps when the voice spoke again.

'Well, now, look who's gonna try to out-Injun me, would you! I'll tell you what, young feller. Why don't you quit bein' scared an' just step on out 'n talk a spell.'

Ike stopped. How had the man heard him? Was he guessing? Who was this?

'Who are you?' he called. 'What do you want?'

'Well, what d'ya know! He talks, too,' the voice responded. 'Now we're gettin' somewhere. My name's Montana Keep. What's yours?'

'Ike Hardy. Fremont County sheriff. You're a ways from Montana.'

'You're a ways from Riverton,' the other responded.

Deciding to trust the man he could not see, Ike holstered his gun and stepped out into the open.

'You always lay up in the brush to scare folks passin' by?' he asked.

He knew he was going to hear a repetition of that cackling laugh, and he was not disappointed. Like a shadow materializing from nothing, a form stepped into sight from a tight cluster of trees.

He was tall. His height was either exaggerated by his being so thin, or he only looked extremely thin because he was so tall. He leaned on a Sharps long rifle. His hawkish face was split by a snaggle-toothed grin.

'You git plumb intent on a trail when you're follerin' it, don't ya?'

Ike felt a flush of indignation rise to his face, then it was replaced by a rush of relief that it was a friendly stranger who had caught him being careless.

'I ain't the world's best tracker. I have to study a trail pretty hard to stay on it. Even so, I'm not usually that careless,' he admitted.

The buckskin-clad mountaineer cackled again. 'I spied on fellers a lot more careful'n you was bein', all right enough,' he said. 'Who're you a-follerin'?'

Ike shook his head. 'They robbed a stage, over by Iron Mountain. Killed a couple people. Shot 'em in cold blood, after they'd already robbed 'em.'

The old-timer chuckled again. 'You

left the saddle like you was shot. I figgered right off you was either a lawman or an outlaw. Pretty much the same, really.'

Ike ignored the barb. 'You live hereabouts?'

'Nosy sort of a feller, ain't ya? Must come from bein' a lawman.'

'Comes from bein' a nosy sort of a feller.'

The man cackled again. 'That's a good answer. Yup. I live in the next valley north o' here. Me'n my woman.'

Ike knew the surprise must have shown on his face. 'You got a family up here?'

'Nope. Just me an' my woman. She's a Shoshone. You in a big hurry?'

'Not particularly.'

'Well, then, you'd jist as well stop by fer a bite to eat.'

Ike hesitated. Then he shrugged. 'I reckon these tracks'll keep,' he said.

'Two.'

'Two what?'

'Take your pick. Two of 'em. They

come through two days ago. Two an' two. See, I know what two an' two is. Turned south just over the mountain.'

'You seen 'em?'

'Nope. Seen their tracks, though. Same day they went through. We'll talk about 'em over a cup o' coffee.'

He picked up the long rifle and let it hang at the end of his right arm. He started easily off through the trees.

Ike mounted his horse and hurried to keep up. It was all the horse could do to keep pace with the lean shadow of a man through the timber.

An hour later they broke out of the timber onto the edge of a small valley. A wisp of smoke rose from a clump of trees at the valley's upper end. He pointed, then led off again. His long legs ate the ground at such a pace Ike's horse had to trot to keep up. In spite of the speed with which he walked, Ike noted he left no tracks and made no sound. It was like following a swift shadow.

Snuggled into the shelter of the trees

was an Indian tepee made of buffalo hides. A tendril of smoke drifted lazily from a fire about ten feet in front of it.

A middle-aged but surprisingly pretty Indian woman worked busily at the fire. She stepped away from the fire and watched their approach without expression. Montana stepped to her side. He said something to her in Indian, then spoke to Ike.

'Ike, this here's my woman, Rain Crow.'

'I am glad to know a beautiful woman of the Shoshone,' Ike said in the same language Montana had used to speak to her.

The Indian woman's eyebrows shot up. 'Welcome to our fire,' she responded.

'You talk Shoshone!' Montana said.

Ike nodded. 'Not real good, but I get by.'

'That so?' the mountaineer replied.

Ike motioned toward Rain Crow. 'Your woman is very pretty.'

Montana looked at his woman with obvious pride. 'She ain't too good with

English, but she understands a heap more'n she lets on,' the mountain man said.

'You trap?' Ike asked, fishing for something to make conversation with.

The man nodded. 'Trap some, hunt some. I take meat down to Fort Laramie, an' to Fort Sanders on south o' there, fer a little cash money, an' ammunition an' such. We scratch out a purty good livin' up here. Where's your badge? I thought lawmen kept a badge out there where it'd ketch the sun an' shine real good.'

'I'm not too keen on being that good a target.'

'Smart, fer a law man. Robbed a stage, huh? Get much?'

Ike shook his head. 'Not much. I 'spect that's why they shot the two they did. Sore about not gettin' much. They seemed to think there'd be a bunch o' money on the stage, and there turned out not to be. You said they turned back south?'

The trapper nodded. 'Looked like

maybe they was headin' back toward where they come from, but not wantin' it to look thataway.'

Ike nodded again. 'I'll trail 'em a ways, an' see if I can find out where they're headin'.'

'Laramie.'

'Laramie?'

'Most likely. Laramie's bigger'n most places. Got a lotta whorehouses an' saloons. Them's the kinda places hold-up men favor. They must be upwards o' three hunert people livin' in Laramie nowdays.'

'It's gettin' big, all right.'

Rain Crow handed them army mess-trays filled with food. They sat down cross-legged on the ground and began to eat. It was good! Ike was not sure what some of the roots and paste were, but it was all tasty. The meat was elk, he was sure.

'Your woman is a very good cook.' Ike said it to Montana, because he understood Indian etiquette, but he said it in Indian for her benefit. He was rewarded with a smile and a proper dropping of her eyes.

The mountaineer only nodded vigorously, his mouth too full to respond.

They put away an enormous amount of food. Rain Crow stood to one side, hands clasped in front of her, and waited for them to finish.

'I finally got her to where she'll eat with me when they's nobody here,' Montana confided. 'But she still won't when anyone else is around. I ain't sure she enjoys it when it's just her'n me. Them Indian customs is hard to break.'

'How'd you come to have an Indian woman?'

'You are nosy, ain't ya? I bought 'er.'

'Bought her?'

'Paid three horses, four buffalo hides, an' two Winchester repeatin' rifles for 'er.'

Ike was at a loss for words. Eventually he said, 'I guess I ain't used to the idea o' buyin' a woman.'

'You oughter know as well as me, that that's the only way you can do, with

44

them people,' Montana asserted. 'Oh, she knowed me. I done asked her if'n she wanted to come with me. It ain't like a slave, or nothin'. But when you gets it all set up betwixt ya, then you got to buy 'er. Shame 'er family if I didn't pay for 'er.'

They ate in silence. The trapper seemed unwilling to drop the subject.

'Ya see, it's like this,' he said at last, 'they ain't no way I'd get me a white woman to come up here an' live an' cook fer me, an' help with the hides an' the huntin' an' all that. An' I ain't content to be alone, no more. Used to be. Not no more.'

'Living alone goes with some men's lives,' Ike responded. 'I got used to the idea a long time ago.'

'Time'll come you won't be used to it no more,' the mountaineer asserted. 'When the nights start gettin' long and cold and lonesome, you start figgerin' how you can get you a woman o' yer own. You'll see.'

They finished their meal in silence.

'Tell you what,' the trapper offered as they rose. 'I got nothin' better to do jist now. Why don't you go on back to Riverton an' mind your own business. I'll track them fellers fer ya, then ride inta town on my buffalo an' let ya know what I found.'

Ike hesitated. 'Your buffalo?'

The trapper nodded, grinning. 'I got me a bull buffalo I done broke to ride. I sorta like ridin' 'im to town onct in a while, fist to watch them smart-alec cowboys try to settle their horses down. He sure kin clear a street, ol' Billy Boy kin. Jist by me a-ridin' in on 'im. Anyhow, I kin track them fellers a sight further'n you kin, I reckon. I'll tell you what I find.'

'You'll come an' tell me, huh?'

'Sure thing. They's a few folks I'd as soon stop an' chin with a spell, anyhow. I knows several folks off thataway. Good to keep in touch, time to time.'

The sheriff thought it over for a long moment. Eventually he nodded, and said:

46

'Much obliged. I'll be ridin' on back, then. Thanks again for the meal.'

He understood the customs. He said nothing to Rain Crow as he rode out.

5

'What in God's green earth is that?'
Theda Sternhagen held a hand over her
eyes to shield them from the sun.

Ira grinned. He squinted at the small
dot on the road, moving toward town.

'Looks like Montana,' he said.

Corky frowned. 'Montana?'

'Haven't you met Montana?' Ira
asked his daughter.

'I been to Montana,' Lonnie responded.

'Not the place, the man,' Ira
corrected. 'Montana Keep, he's called.'

'I've never heard of him.'

'That so? I'm sure I've talked about
him, time to time.'

'Who is he?'

'Oh, he's an old mountain man. Lives
up in the Wind River mountains. Him
and his squaw.'

'Squaw? He married an Indian?'

Ira nodded. 'Shoshone woman. Fine

woman, I think. Don't mix well with white folks, mostly, but then, neither does Montana.'

It was Lonnie's turn to frown. 'I didn't know there were any mountain men around any more.'

'I am just so ashamed,' Ira's mother monotoned from the back seat of the buggy, beside Corky.

Nobody seemed to notice the interruption. 'Not too many,' Ira agreed. 'Montana's gotta be gettin' up there, but I sure wouldn't want him mad at me. He's still a whole lot more man than most men ever were.'

'What does he live on, Papa?'

'I have such good parents,' Ira's mother bemoaned. 'They love me so much. They are going to be so hurt.'

'Oh, he sells furs an' such, mostly. Hunts, and sells the meat to folks. Pretty much lives like the Indians, but alone, just him and his wife.'

'What in the world is he ridin', though?' Lonnie interrupted.

'Oh, that's his buffalo.'

Lonnie and Corky responded as with one voice. 'Buffalo?'

Ira nodded. 'Bull buffalo. You'll see 'im when they get closer. Probably weighs a ton or better.'

'My daddy will come and get me. He will come and take me home. I wouldn't ever let him know what I did, but it's the only way I can get out of here.'

Lonnie ignored the old lady as completely as the rest of them did. The awe in his voice was profound. 'You can break a buffalo to ride?'

'Montana did,' Ira responded. 'Never heard of anyone else doing it. I 'spect he started with 'im as a calf. Most likely bottle-fed him, and kept him away from other buffalo until he was grown. Made a pet out of him.'

'But he broke him to ride?'

'That part wouldn't be all that hard, if he was a pet,' Ira insisted. 'If an animal trusts you, you can train him to do almost anything. I wouldn't be surprised if Montana hadn't taught him to make his coffee.'

'Oh, Papa!' Corky protested.

The dot on the distant road had grown larger as they talked. By now half the people in town seemed to have noticed. A crowd was gathering on the street. A young boy came running along the street as fast as his legs could carry him. 'Pa! Hey, Pa! Come quick! There's a man comin' to town ridin' on a buffalo! He really is, Pa. I ain't lyin'! Come an' look!'

By the time Montana entered the main street, he was the star attraction in a one-ring circus. The street was lined with awed people, gaping in open-mouthed silence. Ira knew Montana was a big man, but he appeared comically small atop the huge animal. Even the saddle looked out of propor-tion, as though a toy had been substituted for a real one. The reins the mountain man held loosely in his hand led down along the sides of the animal's mammoth head, to what must have been a specially made bit in a bridle that would have wrapped twice around any horse's head. Montana grinned, waving at people as his unorthodox mount shambled past.

The horses at the hitch rails were not as awed. They were terrified. All along the street they were squealing and rearing, fighting against the restraints that held them to the hitching rails. Riders were scurrying to grab their horses, trying to calm them before they broke loose and bolted from town entirely. A couple of them did so, racing out of town with reins flying. Unable to succeed, the rest of them were led back between buildings, their owners getting them out of sight of the monstrosity. Lonnie dismounted quickly, wrapping the reins around the top of the wheel of the Sternhagens' buggy, then holding the side-strap as well, crooning to his terrified horse to keep him from bolting with the others.

The grizzled old mountain man spotted Ira, and pulled the reins over to one side. Obediently, as a well-broken saddle horse, the animal swerved at once, heading directly toward the buggy.

At once the team of horses began to toss their heads and prance nervously. Ira crooned to them, reaching up a foot to press the brake-lever just in case their horses also bolted.

'Howdy, Montana,' Ira called.

'Mornin', Ira,' Montana drawled in response. 'Hangin' 'round town 'steada takin' keer o' them critters o' yours, huh?'

Ira grinned. 'That's what I hire all those cowboys for. How've you been standin' the winters?'

'Fair to middlin'. Who's this?'

'This is so embarrassing,' Ira's mother intoned. 'I would rather die than have my parents know what I did. Oh, why did I ever have to do that?'

Ignoring his mother as always, Ira spoke as if he hadn't been interrupted.

'Montana, this is my wife, Theda.'

'Hello, Montana,' Theda said at once.

'Mornin', ma'am. Bit feeble in the head, the old one is, huh?' He turned his attention right back to Ira. 'I met your wife a time 'er two, if'n you remember. Makes a fine cup of coffee. No, I meant who's the purty one?'

Ira turned and looked over his shoulder at his daughter, watching the red creep up her face with delight as he answered. 'I don't guess you've met my daughter, have you? Montana, this is my daughter, Corky.'

Montana snorted. 'Ain't no such thing.'

Ira cocked his head slightly, still smiling. 'Well, her name's Coralee. We call her Corky.'

'Thet ain't what I meant. I meant she ain't your daughter.'

'Why ain't she?'

'Too purty. Way too purty.'

'She took after her mother.'

Montana looked back at Theda, looking her over carefully. 'Well, thet makes sense. I'd done went an' forgot what a handsome woman you married.

Lucky girl, she took after her 'steada you.'

'I can't argue with that.'

The monologue of lonely grief resumed from the back seat of the buggy.

'I won't be here much longer. My parents are coming. My daddy will get me out of here. But they will be so hurt and ashamed.'

Ignoring her as best he could, Montana turned his attention to Lonnie. He was still struggling to keep his horse calmed in the proximity of the buffalo.

'An' this, unless I'm plumb mistook, is the heart-throbbin' cowboy what's got 'is eye on that purty girl o' yours?'

Lonnie and Corky both blushed crimson as everybody grinned at their expense. Lonnie was not at a loss for words, however.

'You just plumb make all kinds o' friends right from the git-go, don't you?' He grinned.

'I jist say what I think, thet's what I

do,' Montana responded.

'Is that why you live way off in the mountains?' Corky asked unexpectedly.

Montana burst into surprised laughter. 'Now thet's callin' 'em straight an' open!' he whooped. 'Yup. Matter o' fact, it is. My mouth jist plumb gits me in trouble around folks, so me'n my woman mostly stay away from folks.'

'So what are you doing in town?' Ira queried.

'Buttin' my nose in where it don't belong.'

'I butted more than my nose in where it didn't belong,' Ira's mother responded.

It was the first time anyone had heard her respond to anything but her own thoughts for a long while. All eyes turned to her. Immediately, however, she resumed her litany of remorse. 'I just don't know why I did anything like that at all. I know better than to do things like that. Oh, why did I have to get caught?'

Ira's eyebrows lifted, but he held his

silence, waiting for the mountain man's explanation. Montana turned his attention back from the old woman.

'I sorta run inta the sheriff up in the edge o' the mountains t'other day. He was tryin' to foller some tracks left by fellas what robbed a stage coach. Kilt a couple folks, he said. Anyhow, he ain't no great shakes at trackin'. I tol' 'im to go on an' mind 'is own business, an' I'd have a go at trackin' 'em, then I'd tell 'im where they went.'

'Did you?'

Montana snorted. ' 'Did I?', the man sez. Ira Sternhagen, you knowed me fer upwards o' twenty years. You know good'n well I kin track a fly acrost granite after dark in a windstorm.'

Ira chuckled. 'Well, I'm not sure you were ever quite that good, but you're getting old, Montana. I didn't know if your eyes were that good any more.'

Montana snorted again. 'My eyes is fine as an eagle's,' he asserted. 'Well, so long's I don't have to look up close. Up close, things is gettin' a mite blurry.

Cain't read no more, cuz my arms ain't long enough. I done read ever'thing I ever wanta read anyhow. And I kin still track jist fine. I may not be quite as good as I used to be, but, the older I get, the better I used to be, so I got room to slip some an' still be the best. Besides, I still ain't bad.'

'Where'd you track 'em to?'

'Your place.'

A gasp escaped the lips of both Theda and Corky. Lonnie grunted as if he had been hit. Ira's brows shot up. 'My ranch?'

Montana nodded. 'Couple o' young fellas. Take big long steps. Ride their horses plumb hard. Went roundabout, some. Right at the edge o' your place they had remounts hid. Switched horses an' rode on. I lost 'em when they hit the main road. Even I cain't track 'em when they mix their tracks inta a hunert others.'

'My ranch,' Ira mused aloud. 'Some of my hands, maybe? What day was the stage robbed?'

'Week ago Monday.'

Ira nodded. 'Well, I'd hate to think it was my hands. In the first place, I'd hate to think Bull was giving any of my hands enough spare time to rob stages, without noticing they were gone.'

'He pushes 'em plumb hard I hear, all right enough,' Montana agreed.

'Even more, I'd sure hate to think any of my hands were thieves and murderers.'

'Cuz they was holdin' their remounts on the edge o' your range, don't mean they was your hands,' Montana reminded him.

Ira sighed heavily. 'Yeah, I know. In fact, I'd say it most likely means they aren't. Still, it's enough to make me worry. When are you going to get yourself an honest riding horse and let that buffalo go make little buffaloes?'

Montana cackled. 'He wouldn't know how to talk to other buffaloes,' he insisted. 'He thinks he's my kid. He don't understand how come ever' horse

59

in town runs away when we come a-ridin' in.'

'Where'd you ever find a saddle to fit him?' Ira asked abruptly.

'Had the saddle-maker up at Casper overhaul one fer me,' Montana replied. 'Wasn't really that tough. Had to make the cinch longer'n wider. That's about all. Sure's a fine animal to ride, though. Smoother'n a horse. In a blizzard, I kin jist give 'im 'is head, an' he'll take us straight home, whether he's gotta face the wind or not. Buffalo weather a storm different from other stock, ya know. They face it, 'stead o' facin' away from it. Got all thet hair, all them heavy brows, an' sich. So Billy Boy here'll walk right inta the face of a blizzard an' take me home, in weather that'd kill a horse.'

'Still don't look natural,' Ira insisted.

'I ain't never been nothin' to look at neither,' Montana said. 'Thisaway they's all a-lookin' at what a strange critter I'm ridin', 'stead o' how ugly I look.'

'I don't think so,' Ira argued at once. 'I don't think anything could do that.'

Their conversation was interrupted. A cowboy, trying to urge his horse down the street past the big bull buffalo lost the battle. The horse had been sidestepping and mincing along. His ears were laid back against his head. His eyes rolled wildly. He champed at the bit feverishly. At the jabbing of his rider's spurs, he kept inching forward until he was exactly even with the huge animal's head. Just then the buffalo tossed his head at the flies buzzing around his eyes. The sudden movement was all the horse needed.

With a squeal, the horse exploded into a frenzy of bucking. The cowboy grabbed the saddle horn and dug his spurs into the cinch strap, toes turned outward. He hauled at the reins, trying to get his horse's head up. He began to curse, first his horse, then the buffalo, in a long blistering tirade as he tried to keep his seat atop the bucking, twisting, terrified mount.

When the horse had bucked a sufficient distance away from the buffalo, he began to feel safer. He stopped bucking, and sidestepped, tossing his head and rolling his eyes, clear onto the board sidewalk. People scattered from his path.

The cowboy cursed again, and jammed spurs to the horse's side. The horse leaped forward, off the sidewalk onto the street, then lunged up the street in a dead run. It took the full length of the street for the cowboy to get the animal under control, and to turn him back to the hitch rail of the saloon. He sat there, considering the situation. He looked at the saloon doors thirstily. He looked back up the street at the mountain man, cackling gleefully atop the buffalo.

Finally he wheeled the horse and rode around the saloon, toward the back. In a few minutes he emerged from the side of the building and ducked into the saloon.

Ira and his family, together with the

mountain man, watched in silence until the cowboy had disappeared into the saloon.

'I bet he'll drink the first couple a mite faster'n he aimed to,' Montana observed.

'And blister your ears while he's doing it,' Ira agreed.

Montana grinned. 'That's a fact. Wal, I gotta go tell the sheriff what I found, an' head back fer my mountain. This here civilization ain't no place fer me. Me'n Billy Boy's jist gonna get in trouble here.'

'Well, you take care of yourself,' Ira responded. 'Stop by the ranch any time you get a chance. Coffee-pot's always on.'

Lifting a hand, Montana tipped his greasy hat to the ladies and kicked his mount into motion, heading for the sheriff's office.

'Don't leave yet, Papa,' Corky said suddenly. 'I want to see how he gets on and off that beast.'

Obediently, Ira waited and watched,

half-listening to the continuing monologue from his mother in the back seat
of the buggy. Montana stopped the
buffalo bull in front of the sheriff's
office. He reached behind him and
unfastened something they could not
see. He flipped a rope down that had
been draped up across the back of his
saddle. It had two loops attached to it.
Its other end was secured to the saddle.
Drawing his right foot across the back
of the saddle, Montana stepped downward. He thrust his toe into one of the
loops on that rope. Then he pulled his
left foot out of the stirrup and stepped
down to stick it into the second loop on
the rope. Then he removed the right
foot from its loop and stepped to the
ground.

'It's a ladder!' Corky squealed.

Ira grinned, choosing not to answer
as he picked up the reins and nudged
his team into motion.

6

The sun reflected one quick, brilliant flash. It was enough. Ira nodded, and turned back from watching the approaching rider. He gave his attention back to the round corral.

'Don't let 'er up, Puke! Jump in there an' get a knee on her neck while she's down.'

Knowing what was coming, every hand at the ranch was perched on the top rail of the corral. Their air of expectancy awaited the day's entertainment.

Puke Granger had successfully front-footed a raw bronc. Freshly brought in off the range, the horse had never felt a rope nor been in a corral. As he ran in a circle, seeking escape from the young cowboy, Puke had whirled his rope slowly until he had the position and timing he wanted. Then he cast his loop, turning his wrist as he did so. The loop sailed out in front of the fleeing horse, and turned over just in front of his front feet. Unable to stop his momentum, the horse had stepped into the loop with both of those feet. Instantly Puke hauled on the rope, tightening the noose around both front hocks. The result was the immediate crashing to the ground of the big bay mare.

Responding to his boss's urging, he sprinted to the prone horse, already struggling to rise. He grabbed an ear, forcing her head back to the ground. Then he knelt with a knee on her neck, just behind the head. Try as she might, she could do nothing. She could not stand, with his weight on her neck. She could not kick him. She could only struggle, her eyes rolling wildly, her breath coming in great snorts.

'Lonnie, take him a hackamore, now,' Ira called.

Already moving before the instructions came, Lonnie crossed the corral with a hackamore. Keeping his knee on the horse's neck, Puke arranged the hackamore and fastened it on the horse's head, leaving the reins to trail on the ground.

'Want me to tie up a foot?' Puke called.

'Sure,' Ira responded.

Puke reached back for the end of his lariat that he had dropped on the ground. Pulling it free from beneath the horse's head, he flipped it several times to loosen the loop around the horse's front feet. As soon as the mare felt it loosen, she began flailing with those feet. That action, together with the slack Puke fed into the rope, allowed her to get her feet free of the loop.

Puke took the other end of the rope and worked it under the horse's neck, without allowing her enough freedom to get up. Then he tied it in a bowline knot that would not pull tight on her neck. Then he flipped the rope so it would encircle one hind foot. Looping it around that leg, between the hoof and hock, he tied it back to the loop he had made around her neck.

'Now you can let 'er up,' Ira called.

Obediently, Puke removed his weight from the horse's neck, stood up, and backed up a step. The horse responded immediately. She hauled herself erect, only to find that one hind leg was now held two feet off the ground. On three legs, she could neither kick nor run. She jerked the bound leg frantically for several minutes, before realizing she could not free it.

Leaving her to stand there, Puke walked over to the edge of the corral and picked up a saddle and blankets. He carried them to the horse and dropped them on the ground. He brushed the horse carefully where the saddle would go, to be sure no barbs or burrs were embedded in her hair that would poke or gouge her once the saddle was on. Then he spread the blankets carefully on her back.

As he did, the mare snorted and squirmed, trying again to free the bound hind foot. Her ears were laid back tightly against her head. Her eyes rolled wildly. Her breath came in gasps that sounded like something between squeals and growls.

'Don't get where she can bite you,' Ira called. 'I don't want 'er to get started doin' that at all.'

Puke glanced over his shoulder to make sure he was out of reach of her attempts, but did not otherwise acknowledge the instructions. He picked up the saddle and set it gently on the mare's back. As soon as the weight settled on her, the mare again went through a fit of squirming and jerking, almost falling in her efforts to free the bound leg so she could fight this terrifying new menace.

Ignoring her struggles, Puke cinched the saddle down tight. Then he fed the reins of the hackamore along either side of her neck, and took hold of both. He pulled his hat down tightly onto his head until it was wedged right at the top of his eyebrows. He stuck his foot in the stirrup and stepped lightly into the saddle. The mare squealed in fear and anger as his weight settled onto her back. She swung her head back and forth in a vain effort to reach his legs or feet. She nearly fell again, trying to get her hind leg out of the constricting rope.

'Let 'er stand a minute, to get used to your weight,' Ira said.

After a few minutes the mare settled down, and Ira spoke again. 'Take the rope off her neck now, Lonnie. Untie it so it'll come clear off when it comes loose. I don't want that rope hanging there for her to get tangled in when she blows up.'

Already moving to obey, Lonnie undid the bowline knot and removed the loop from the mare's neck, while he held the hind foot off the ground with a solid grip on the ropes leading to it. When the rest of the rope was free, he let loose of one of the ropes leading to the foot, and pulled the loop loose, freeing the captive leg.

The mare kicked twice with that leg, as if to assure herself it was really free now. Then she stood, trembling, for several heartbeats. Then she squealed and leaped into the air, ducking her head between her front legs, twisting in mid-jump to try to unseat the unwelcome presence on her back. She came down with all four legs together, sending a jarring jolt through Puke. He felt as if his head were being driven clear down through his shoulders.

The instant her feet hit the ground, the mare ran two jumps forward, then began to buck in earnest. She bucked and squealed and kicked her way around the corral in a growing cloud of dust. Puke leaned back in the saddle and wedged his knees as tightly as he could beneath the swells on the pommel of his saddle. He turned his toes outward, digging his spurs into the rope strands of the cinch to help hold himself in the saddle.

'Better pull leather, Puke,' a hand called from atop the corral fence.

'She's gonna get the best of you, Puke,' another called.

'Aw, you got 'er rode,' another disagreed. 'Relax an' enjoy the ride.'

'By Jing, you might be a bronc stomper after all, Puke.'

'Look at 'er sunfish! Don't let that belly-roll loosen you, Puke.'

For ten minutes that seemed like ten hours, the horse tried everything her instincts had endowed her with to unseat the rider. It was all to no avail. He sat the saddle as if glued to it. She stopped bucking and began to run. She would run directly toward the corral fence, turning at the last possible moment to avoid a collision. Then she would run to the other side of the corral and do the same. Each time, as she approached the fence, Puke hauled the reins one direction or the other, forcing her to turn the direction he chose. She didn't even realize she was already being taught to neck-rein.

Then she abruptly stopped. She stood, spraddle-legged, in the middle of

72

the corral. Her sides heaved. Her breath came in ragged gasps. Slobbers drooled from her open mouth.

'Talk to 'er,' Ira called. 'Let 'er know it's all right. Then nudge 'er some and get her moving.'

Puke at once began to croon to the mare, even as he nudged her gently with his spurs. At his first touch of the spurs, she squealed and bucked again, half-heartedly. Then she tossed her head, trotted about twenty feet, and stopped.

As soon as she stopped, Puke nudged her again. He moved her around the corral for a good thirty minutes. After the first five minutes or so, she began to respond to the reins.

'She's gonna break plumb easy,' a cowboy commented.

'She's takin' to it all right,' another agreed.

Ira spoke again. 'Grab the hackamore, Lonnie. Let Puke get off and on a dozen or so times, then you boys can unsaddle her and get her rubbed down.

Give her a good bait of oats. Let 'er get the idea that there's a real fine treat waiting when she gets ridden. She'll remember that. I got to go talk to the sheriff.'

Ike Hardy chuckled behind Ira. 'I wondered if I could ride into the ranch yard and not have anyone notice. I shoulda knowed better.'

Ira grinned, holding out his hand. 'I saw the sun flash off of that badge when you were down by the big cottonwood.'

Ike took the hand and shook it firmly and warmly. 'Good to see you, Ira.'

'I figured you'd be around,' Ira responded.

Ike's brows raised. 'That so?'

'We run into Montana Keep in town yesterday. He told me he tracked those stage robbers roundabout and back onto my range.'

Ike nodded, but did not speak.

'I 'spect you'll be wantin' to quiz Bull some on where all of our hands were, last Monday.'

Ike nodded again. 'If you boys ain't too busy.'

'Come on into the house. I'm sure Theda's got the coffee-pot on. If not, it won't take her long to make some.'

He turned back to the corral. 'Hey, Bull. You want to come on up to the house?'

'Be right there,' Bull responded. Then he turned to the rest of the hands. 'You boys had your show for the day. You all got work needs done. Get to it. If anyone doesn't have anything to do, the barn could use a good cleanin'.'

Every hand suddenly remembered some chores that demanded immediate attention. The corral fence cleared within seconds.

The inside of the big ranch house felt cool, away from the glare of the midday sun. The three men paused inside the door, letting their eyes adjust to the dimmer light.

'Why, hello, Ike,' Theda greeted him. 'The coffee's on in the kitchen. Have you eaten?'

'Yeah,' the sheriff responded. 'Just a cup of coffee would be fine. Unless, of course, there happens to be some of your spice-cake sittin' around gettin' stale.'

'Just happen to have some,' Theda responded.

The three sat at the table. As though in repetition of some ancient ritual, each man laid his hat on the floor beside his chair, turned upside down so its weight would not change the angle the brim had been carefully trained to maintain. Theda placed cups on the table and filled them with steaming black coffee. Then she placed a plate containing a huge piece of russet-colored cake, topped with white frosting, beside each cup. She laid forks on the table, then turned to Ira.

'If you need anything else, holler. I'll be in the other room.'

The three murmured their thanks as she left the room. As soon as she was gone, Ira said, 'Bull, I didn't tell you. When we was in town yesterday,

Montana Keep rode in.'

'On a horse, or on that buffalo of his?'

'On Billy Boy.'

'Bet that raised a ruckus in town,' Bull chuckled.

'It did create a little excitement,' the sheriff acknowledged.

Ira picked up the conversation. 'Montana told me he'd been doing a little tracking for the sheriff. There was a stage hold-up along the gas hills road. They didn't get much, but they killed two people. They went up over the pass, then roundabout and back here. Had remounts tied in the willows at the swamp on the north edge of our range.'

'Came back here!' Bull responded. 'You think it was some of our hands?'

The sheriff took a sip of the scalding black liquid before he answered. 'Could be,' he acknowledged. 'They knew where they could leave their remounts, where they wouldn't be found. Then they just turned loose the ones they'd been ridin'.'

Ira started visibly. 'Montana didn't tell me that!' he said. 'Left 'em there?'

The sheriff nodded. 'They hung around, eatin', drinkin' outa the crick, Montana said, for several hours. Then they wandered off, but didn't seem to be in any hurry to go anywhere.'

'Like they were on their home range,' Bull mused.

Ike nodded. 'Montana didn't follow 'em. Followed the new horses, but not too far. They hit the main road and mixed their tracks into everyone else's, so they couldn't be followed any more, just in case they were tracked.'

Ira sighed heavily. 'I was sure hopin' it was just somebody that chanced to leave their horses there, but weren't from around here. I just assumed they led the extras along with 'em when they left, and didn't even ask. Well, Bull, what hands did we have that could've been gone that long without being missed last Monday?'

Bull stared at the ceiling, mentally picturing the day in question. 'I can't think of any. Two, you say? We had two men off to town after oats an' such, but they wasn't late gettin' back.'

'I checked them boys out already,' the sheriff said. 'They was in town when the stage was bein' robbed. They're clean.'

'I can't think of any others,' Bull admitted. 'That's a far piece to ride and end up back here. They'd have to ride thirty miles.'

'That's about what I figured,' the sheriff agreed. 'I'd particularly like to know about a couple o' your hands.'

'Which two?'

'Arn Banning and Wes Ulger.'

Bull grunted. 'If there was something goin' on like that, they're the first two I'd check out, too. But I don't think it coulda been them. I sent them out to check on the heifers that're clear up past the Thompson Rim. That's the opposite direction, and they couldn't do that and any more than just get back by dark. I don't think there's any way it could've been them.'

The sheriff was visibly disappointed. 'Any other ideas?'

'Not a one,' admitted Bull. 'I can watch and listen. See if any of the hands seem to have extra money. See if any of 'em are curious about what you wanted. That sorta thing. I don't know anything else to offer.'

'Good enough.' The sheriff sighed. 'I'll be ridin' on back to town. Let me know if you think of anything. Oh, you might watch for a real nice gold watch. The driver said one of the fellers that got shot had given up a real fine watch. Gold chain and all. If somebody comes up with a new watch, let me know.'

Ira watched the sheriff ride out of the yard. He felt like something heavy and raw lay in the pit of his stomach.

7

'They are majestic birds, ain't they?'

Corky jumped, startled at the voice behind her. She whirled to see Arn Banning grinning at her. 'Oh, Arn! You startled me! I didn't even hear you ride up.'

'I noticed you was plumb engrossed in watching your favorite eagles.'

'They are majestic,' she agreed. 'So big and beautiful. They've been having a running battle with the squirrels in their tree all spring.'

'That's why they don't usually nest in trees,' he explained wisely. 'They go more for crags on the cliff faces an' such. I don't know why they chose that tree.'

'I don't either, but they shouldn't have.'

'Why not?'

'Because I think the squirrels won.'

'They get to the eggs?'

'I think so. The eagles are acting like it, and they don't stay on the nest at all now.'

'That so? I wonder if they'll mate again this year?'

'I don't know,' she replied. 'I don't know if they mate more than once a year.'

'That'd be a terrible life,' he observed.

'What would? Being able to fly like an eagle?'

'No, that'd be fine. I mean the part about only bein' able to mate once a year.'

She giggled. 'Arn! Watch your tongue. This is mixed company, you know.'

'I was more aware of that than you know,' he responded.

She felt herself turn red, but declined to answer.

'Look at there!' Arn pointed.

One of the eagles had folded its wings and was diving toward the ground. Their eyes jerked toward the ground, as if controlled by some same, hidden string. On the ground, about twenty feet from the edge of the trees, one of the squirrels scampered about, searching for food among the edges of the grass.

They looked back up, watching the eagle darting from the sky with incredible speed, toward the unsuspecting squirrel.

'Revenge time,' Arn gloated.

'Oh!' was all Corky could say.

Some primal instinct maybe. Some unheard warning from one of its fellows in the trees perhaps. An accidental glance skyward possibly. Whatever it was, something prompted the squirrel to abruptly abandon its search for food and scamper for the protection of the overhanging trees.

The dive of the eagle missed it by inches as it scurried away. The eagle rose back into the sky on the lift of its majestic wings.

'Oh, that was so close!' Corky said.

'He musta spotted 'im from all the way up there, an' thought it was his chance to get even. Spotted that big ol' tail a switchin' around, most likely.'

'It seems impossible that he could see him from that far up. And then dive that far, that accurately. If he hadn't run just when he did, he'd have been dead.'

'He almost had 'im,' Arn agreed. 'Six inches. He couldn'ta missed him more'n six inches. You wasn't rootin' for the squirrel, was you?'

'I don't know,' Corky admitted. 'When they were after the eggs, I was hoping the eagles would kill them. Then when the eagle was diving, I was hoping he would escape. I don't know why.'

'You need to make up your mind which side you're on,' Arn remonstrated.

After a moment of awkward silence, he said, 'Let's wander down there by the tree. See if we can see them squirrels.'

'Why?'

'Oh, I don't know. Maybe we can weigh in on the eagles' side a bit.'

Frowning, she rose from the ground. He grabbed her hand to help her up. Then he held on to it, instead of releasing it when she was standing. A tingle from his touch shuddered its way through her, making her at once a little excited and a little afraid. She gently pulled her hand away from his, and started down the hill.

They were half-way to the trees when she noticed he was carrying something.

'What are you carrying?' she asked.

He grinned. 'I wrapped up a little lunch. I saw you ride outa the yard, an' figgered this might be where you was goin'. I had a little time on my hands, so I just thought I'd rig up a little picnic lunch an' bring up here for you. I talked to Cookie, an' he let me have some stuff. We can find us a nice spot down there in the trees an' eat it in the shade.'

A sudden surge of apprehension shot through her. She glanced back at her horse, ground-tied beside Arn's. She looked at the dense timber they were heading for, feeling somehow ill at ease to be enclosed, away from anyone's view in there with Arn.

Uncertain how to voice her misgivings without directly insulting Arn or his intentions, she continued down the hill. His casual chatter began to allay her fears, and she pushed the qualms from her mind.

The timber was cool and quiet, away from the bright glare of the Wyoming sun. Arn was leading now, and she followed, responding to his gaiety with chatter of her own. They emerged from the thick timber into a large clearing. Almost in the center stood the huge spruce tree the eagles had claimed for their aerie. They both stopped and craned their necks to look up into its lofty heights. 'That is one big tree,' Arn breathed.

'It's magnificent,' Corky agreed. 'I didn't realize how big it is, watching it from the ridge all the time.'

'Can't even see the top,' Arn observed.

'Not very well,' she concurred.

'Shh! Hold still,' he whispered.

'What is it?' she answered, whispering as softly as she could.

'The squirrels is down low on the trunk,' he whispered back. 'Don't make a sound, maybe I can get a shot at 'em.'

They stood there together in total silence, scarcely daring to breathe. They could hear the chatter of the squirrels, but were not able to see them. Then they emerged into view, scuttling around the trunk of the great tree.

Just as Corky glanced over at Arn, his hand streaked to his gun. In a blur of motion he swept the gun from its holster, firing as it came level, then firing again so swiftly the two shots sounded as one.

Corky whipped her eyes back to the tree just in time to see both squirrels tumble to the ground. 'Got 'em both!' Arn exulted.

'Wow! That was some shooting!'

Corky breathed.

'Good, ain't I?' Arn boasted. 'I bet you didn't know I could shoot like that.'

'No, I didn't,' she admitted. 'Where did you learn that?'

'Been practicin' all my life,' he informed her. 'C'mon.'

'What are you doing?'

'Gettin' the pretty lady a prize,' he said.

He strode to where the two squirrels lay dead. They laid in the thick carpet of dead spruce needles, piled from countless years of the tree's shedding them. He pulled a knife from its sheath at his belt, and cut off the long, bushy tails of both squirrels. He carried them back to Corky. 'Let's put 'em on our hats,' he said.

'On our hats?'

'Sure. Like this.'

He removed his hat and took a piece of string out of his pocket. He tied the string firmly around the upper end of one of the squirrel-tails. Then he fastened it to the back of his hatband.

When he put it back on, the long squirrel's tail dangled off the back brim of his hat.

'Now let me do yours,' he said.

'No!' Corky protested. 'I don't want that thing on my hat! It'll start to stink in a day or two. It's not even tanned or anything.'

'Naw, they don't never stink,' he disagreed. 'I've done 'em before. They just dry up. Let me put it on your hat, then we'll be a matched pair.'

'No! I really don't want it on my hat. Come on. We'd better go.'

'Go? But we just got here. And I got this great lunch I brought out here, just for us. You and me.'

Her heart pounded in her ears. The sense of his presence towered over her, sending emotions she had never felt coursing through her. The sense of isolation within the walls of timber suddenly felt more threatening than exciting to her.

'OK,' she said. 'We'll eat. But let's go back up by the horses. It's . . . it's too chilly here in the trees.'

'Oh, but I really like it here in the trees,' he protested. 'It's so quiet and private and everything.'

'I know, but it's really chilly,' she repeated. 'Come on. Let's go back up on the grass and eat.'

It seemed to her to take forever to retrace their way through the trees to the open sunlight. When they emerged into its bright glare it felt as if a great weight was lifted from her. She smiled radiantly at Arn.

'See how nice it is out here?'

'Plumb bright,' Arn complained.

'So what did you bring for us to eat?'

Almost reluctantly he spread out the lunch he had brought. Corky kept up a running conversation while they ate, but Arn said little. As soon as they had finished, she said, 'That was really nice, Arn. Thank you. I really do have to get back to the ranch, though. Are you going to ride back with me?'

Half a dozen emotions crossed his face in rapid sequence before he answered, 'Naw, I guess not. I'm supposed to be findin' a couple bulls that wandered up this direction. I'd best get 'em found and haze 'em back down where they belong. We'll come back up here another time, though, when we got more time. OK?'

'Sure,' she said, a little too offhandedly. 'I'll see you back at the ranch.'

She mounted quickly and rode away at a swift trot. Arn stood on the ridge for a long while, watching her ride away.

Arn was still in a strange and sour mood when he rode into the ranch yard at supper time. He joined the line-up of cowboys washing up in the basin behind the cookhouse.

'Boy, that Corky sure is a lot of woman,' he commented.

Several of the hands glanced at him, but none made any remark. He pursued the issue. 'I sure do aim to make that little filly my woman,' he continued. 'She's a woman that could keep a man warm on the worst night of winter.'

That time his comments did not go unchallenged.

'Leave her alone. She ain't your type.'

Arn turned to see who dared to challenge him. Lonnie Bursell stood glaring at him.

Arn grinned. 'Well, pretty boy! What's the matter? You figure you got that territory all staked out for yourself, do you?'

'That's none of your business,' Lonnie retorted. 'But you don't, and you won't. If I catch you anywhere near Corky I'll nail your hide to the wall.'

Arn's grin widened. 'Well, listen to pretty boy. I'll tell you what, big man: if you think you're man enough to nail my hide to the wall this is just as good a time as any to prove it.'

He never saw Lonnie's fist coming until it flattened his nose, sending blood spewing across Arn's face. Arn took a step backward, but didn't lose his footing. He roared in anger and pain and charged, swinging, toward the cowboy.

Lonnie quickly sidestepped, sending a chopping hook into the side of Arn's face as he went by. The blow sent Arn sprawling off the porch on to the ground. He bounced to his feet at once.

Lonnie stepped off the porch to meet the rush of the wounded swain and caught a straight right to the chin which jarred him. He shook it off and countered with a left that connected with Arn's right cheek.

They stood there, toe to toe, slugging with all their might, as the crew gathered in a circle to watch. Lonnie stopped swinging at the other man's face and sent three hard blows in a row into his midsection. He grunted at the first blow, gasped at the second, and took a full step backward at the third.

Lonnie followed with a straight left to Arn's already shattered nose, then crossed with a right that connected solidly with his jaw. Arn went to his knees. Lonnie stepped forward, sending an underhand left into Arn's face that toppled him over backward.

Without a word, Lonnie turned and walked back up on the porch and began to wash up. The water in the basin quickly turned blood red, as Lonnie cleaned and explored his wounds.

'Don't try it!' The barking voice of Bull Whetstine froze everybody in their tracks.

Turning, Lonnie saw Arn standing unsteadily, his legs spraddled wide. His hand was on his gun, already halfway out of the holster. Bull stood with a double-barreled shotgun trained on the cowboy's chest.

'I ain't gonna have any shootin' amongst the crew!' Bull barked. 'Put it away and leave it there. You boys want to beat on each other, that's your business, but keep it to your fists. Understood?'

Arn glared at the foreman for a long moment, obviously weighing his chances against the shotgun and knowing they were somewhere between slim and none. Finally he jammed the gun back down into the holster. Muttering under his breath, he stumbled up onto the porch and began washing up in another of the wash-basins.

Speaking softly, Bull said, 'He ain't likely to forget that, Lonnie.'

'He ain't likely to forget your shotgun, either. Thanks.'

Both men knew the warning was well spoken. Neither man knew how strongly it bore heeding.

8

'Hey, Cowgirl. Want to ride with me today?'

Corky's smile was quick. 'With you, sure! Anytime. Where are we riding?'

Lonnie gestured with a broad sweep of his hand. 'Bull wants me to ride up an' check on them first-calf heifers. I ain't sure why. He just sent Arn and Wes up to check on 'em last Monday. I guess that has been a week.'

'That's a long ride. It's clear past the Thompson Rim, isn't it?'

'Yup. It'll take a long day, even if we don't run into anything that takes work.'

'I'll pack us a lunch, then.'

'Sounds good to me. Want me to saddle Belle?'

'No. Saddle Sugar for me. He's got more bottom for a long day.'

'You got it. You best check with your

pa. Make sure it's OK with him.'

She started to say something, then thought better of it. She did mutter to herself as she strode to the house.

Half an hour later they rode out of the ranch yard, riding stirrup to stirrup. They chattered happily about everything and nothing for the two hours.

Then Lonnie said, 'We'd best pick up the pace. We're gonna be all day just a-gettin' there.'

Acting in almost perfect concert, they touched their horses with the spurs. The horses responded by breaking into a swift, ground-eating trot. Riding a fast trot took more energy and made conversation more difficult, so they rode in silence until they were passing below the Thompson Rim. There, Corky gestured without slowing her horse.

'That's the big ol' spruce where the eagles are nested.'

'I seen 'em both flyin' around,' Lonnie responded. 'There's one of 'em now.' He pointed, and she followed the direction he indicated. A bald eagle appeared to float effortlessly on an air thermal. His great wings were outspread, but unmoving. He turned slowly, seeming to hang suspended in space.

'They are so beautiful,' Corky said.

'They are some bird!' Lonnie agreed. 'Look! He's spotted somethin'!'

As they watched, the eagle folded his wings. He thrust his head down and forward. His body became a pointed projectile, sleek and slender. As it fell, it picked up speed until it was traveling at an alarming rate. Like a meteor he shot earthward. At the last moment, he spread his massive wings and swooped, nearly touching the ground. In his talons as he swept upward was the limp body of a cottontail rabbit.

'Wow!' Corky breathed. 'That rabbit never knew what hit it.'

'Never felt a thing,' Lonnie agreed. 'Them talons hit so hard I bet they drove plumb through it. Even if they didn't, a blow like that would kill a rabbit instantly.'

'He's taking it to the nest,' Corky pointed.

Lonnie nodded. Neither was aware they had reined in their horses. They sat there together, spellbound by the drama nature performed before them. As the eagle landed on the nest, the other eagle joined it. They began tearing the carcass of the dead rabbit to pieces.

Both Lonnie and Corky were suddenly intensely aware that they were sitting, stirrup to stirrup, holding hands as they watched. She did not remember reaching out to grab his hand as the eagle plummeted to the ground. He, on the other hand, noticed it with great delight. He was only too glad to interlace his fingers with hers, to feel the closeness of her, to see the excitement bubble in her as she watched. He nearly forgot to watch the eagle, for watching her.

As she became aware they were holding hands, she felt herself blush.

She started to withdraw her hand, then thought better of it. It felt right and good, somehow, and she didn't want to break the spell. They both pretended to stare at the eagles they could no longer see within the nest.

After several minutes, she said, 'We better get going.'

'Do we have to?' Lonnie asked.

Corky giggled. 'I think we better,' she replied. 'We may forget what we're supposed to be doing.'

'I could do that real easy with you,' he surprised himself by saying.

Her eyes danced and sparkled. 'And if it takes us too long to check those heifers, Papa will peel your hide off, asking what we were doing for so long.'

'You got a point there,' Lonnie admitted. 'I can't say that I blame him. If you were mine, I don't think I'd let you out of my sight.'

'Then I'm glad I'm not yours,' she rejoined. 'I like my freedom too much to have someone keeping track of me all the time. Come on.'

She released his hand and touched the spurs to her horse. They resumed their course, still riding stirrup to stirrup, still very much aware of each other's presence.

It was another hour and a half before they descended into the broad meadow where the heifers were grazing. Grass and water were abundant, and there was no reason for them to wander, so they could be trusted to remain within that small valley for the duration of the summer.

They could make out nearly a hundred head of the young cows, grazing contentedly, or lying in the tall grass chewing their cuds. They sat there together, drinking in the beauty of the valley.

Small springs seeped and ran into trickles of water from two dozen places in the valley. The trickles joined together, one by one, until they became a stream, meandering along through tall grass and brush. Raspberry and plum bushes grew in profusion along its banks. Beyond the valley, rocky peaks jutted up in a variety of colors, broken by streaks of green, where either timber or grass reached for greater heights. Above them, the tall peaks, deeply covered with snow, glistened against the blue sky.

Lonnie spoke, breaking the spell. 'Let's eat lunch over there by the spring. Then we can ride a circle around the valley, make sure everything's okay. There's bear up here, but they don't bother stock much. They will if they get hungry, but they got lots to eat. Cougars would be more of a danger. Mostly, there ain't much up here that'd hurt stock. Not even rattlers up here for 'em to get snakebit by.'

'There aren't any snakes here?'

'Nope. We're above the snake line. They don't like it too high up.'

'I wonder why.'

'Don't know. About the level of the rim is as high as you ever see any.'

They found a large rock beside the spring. They sat down side by side on the grass, and leaned back against the rock. They ate in almost total silence, as they drank in the beauty of the land. When they finished, they washed their hands in the trickle of water spilling out of the ground, across a rock, then falling some three feet into a small pool.

Corky peered at Lonnie from under her hat-brim, waiting for him to get in the right position. As he did, she slapped her hand through the trickle of water, sending a shower of the ice-cold liquid fully into his face.

Lonnie yelped in surprise and jumped back. Then he grinned. 'Why you ornery little pup! I'll wash your face in that!'

He grabbed her, with an arm around her neck, holding her tightly against himself. As she squealed and struggled, he dragged her toward the spring. When they were close enough, he reached his free hand out, cupped, into the stream of water. As she squealed and squirmed, he brought the handful of ice-water and wiped it across her face.

What he didn't notice was that, as he was doing that, she used a free hand to take off her hat. As she pretended to try to squirm away from him, she was holding her hat, upside down, beneath the spring's flow. When Lonnie decided he had her face sufficiently wet, he released her.

Instead of stepping back away from him, Corky stayed tightly against him. She reached up and jerked his hat from his head, then dumped the hatful of spring water she had collected into her hat over his head.

Lonnie gasped with shock and whooped as the icy liquid covered his head and poured down his neck. Corky ran away, laughing, with Lonnie in hot pursuit. They climbed across the rocks above the spring and started down the other side, when Corky stopped abruptly. Lonnie almost knocked her down, but managed to stop. It was not entirely without being aware of what he was doing that he slipped an arm around her waist to steady himself.

'What is it?' he asked.

She pointed to the bottom of the valley, just below them. 'Look,' she said. 'There's a dead calf. But I can't tell what that is by it.'

He squinted, holding his hand to shield his eyes, since his hat still lay beside the spring. The laughter left his face. His mouth straightened to a thin line. His eyes narrowed.

'Looks like a heifer bogged down an' died,' he said quietly.

'Bogged down? I didn't know it was boggy up here.'

'There's always boggy spots where there's always water,' he said. 'We best check it out.'

They turned and scrambled across the rocks, climbing back down to where they had lunched. He retrieved his hat while Corky picked up the remains of their lunch and stuffed it in her saddle-bag. They mounted and rode out without a word.

At the bottom of the valley they rode into a putrid stench that grew with every step of the horses.

'I hate the smell of dead animals,' Corky complained.

'Purty bad all right,' Lonnie agreed. 'Been dead a while.'

'How long?'

Lonnie didn't answer until they had ridden right up to the dead pair. The heifer was in a deep mud hole that she had wandered into, and had been unable to find anything solid enough to step on, to allow her to get out again. She had wallowed around in the thick mud that came up half-way on her side until she had finally died. Unable to fend for himself, her calf waited helplessly, as close as he could get to her, until he died of starvation.

'She's been dead a week and a half,' Lonnie said. 'Maybe two weeks. Her calf's only been dead a day or so.'

'The poor thing!' Corky cried. 'He just waited and waited, and starved to death. It's a wonder something didn't come along and kill him before that.'

'It is for a fact,' Lonnie agreed. 'A

bear, or a cougar, or a coyote, or 'most anything. Wolf even. You'da sure thought something would've found him afore he just starved to death.'

'Did you say she's been dead over a week?' Corky remembered. 'I wonder why Arn and Wes didn't notice her.'

'That's what I was wonderin',' Lonnie agreed. 'Her calf shoulda been bawlin' his head off about the time they was up here. Well, there ain't nothin' we can do for either one of 'em. Let's check out the rest of the bunch.'

'Oh, Lonnie! Is that another one?'

Following the direction of her point, Lonnie saw a dark splotch at the edge of another swampy area. He lifted his reins and nudged his horse into a trot. There, another heifer's body bore witness to the same tragedy. The boggy area around the heifer was now dried enough to be merely spongy, rather than the bog-hole that had claimed her life.

'She had to've been alive last

Monday,' Lonnie muttered. 'She ain't been dead that long, and it would've taken her several days to die. She was bogged down, sure as sin, when they was up here. No sign of her calf.'

'Maybe that's why nothing ate the other calf,' Corky offered. 'Maybe whatever is around was full from this one.'

Riding a growing series of circles around the dead heifer, Lonnie soon rode on to the remains of the missing calf.

'It's over here,' he called back to Corky.

As she rode up beside him, he pointed to the torn remains of the small body. 'Wolves,' he said. 'See the tracks in the soft spots. Three or four of 'em. Didn't leave much.'

'Well, at least he didn't have to starve to death,' she sighed.

'Come on,' Lonnie said, sounding more gruff than he wanted to. 'Let's get the rest of 'em checked out.'

Half an hour later they spotted

another heifer in trouble. She was in a boggy spot almost identical to the ones that had claimed the other two. Riding as close as he could get, Lonnie threw a loop from his lariat over her head. Drawing it tight, he turned his horse and began dragging her from the mud. At first she fought the rope and resisted. Then, as she began to move, she began to try to flail her way out of the soupy mire. By the time Lonnie had pulled her twice her own length, she began to find firmer ground beneath her feet. She stumbled on to dry ground and stood, spraddle-legged, gasping for air.

Lonnie rode closer, shaking his rope to loosen the loop around her neck. As he did, the heifer shook her head, tossing the loop aside. Lonnie recoiled it, grumbling aloud about the mud that clung to his rope.

They rode fifty yards away and stopped to watch. A bawling calf approached the mud encrusted cow. 'He better start suckin' purty quick,'

Lonnie observed.

'Why?' Corky wondered.

'If he waits very long, the mud that's all over her tits is gonna start gettin' dry, an' he won't be able to get through it.'

'But he's going to get an awful mouthful of mud!' she observed.

'He is that,' Lonnie agreed. 'Can't be helped. Unless you can persuade her to go over by a spring an' stand real still while you warsh 'er off.'

Corky giggled. 'I think I'll just let him taste a little mud,' she said.

The calf nuzzled up beside his mother and began trying to suck. He grabbed a teat and immediately backed away, shaking his head. Hunger overwhelmed distaste for the mud immediately, however. He went back for more, and again backed off, shaking his head. The third time he stayed, and began filling his stomach.

He had just gotten started good when the heifer kicked, shoving the calf away.

'Why did she do that?' Corky wondered.

Lonnie shrugged. 'Just outa sorts, most likely. Wonder she's lettin' him suck at all. Sometimes, you pull 'em out of a bog thataway, they'll take after you.'

'I know. Papa told me that, and I saw an old cow do that to him once. She couldn't even stand up when he got her pulled out of the mud. He tailed her up, then she chased him back to his horse, like it was his fault she got bogged down.'

'They'll do it.'

As they talked, the calf resumed his efforts to fill his stomach. He failed to get hold of the teat he had already cleaned, however, and went through the same process of mud removal before settling down to suck.

'Let's ride,' Lonnie said, lifting his reins. 'They'll be fine.'

Before they had completed their circuit of the valley, they found one more heifer that had bogged down and

111

died. There, too, the bog had dried enough for it to be no longer a hazard to livestock. It accentuated the question of why two hands riding the same circuit had failed to find that many cows in trouble.

They spurred their horses to that swift, ground-eating trot and headed back for the TS Bar. They spoke little on the long ride back to the ranch, content just to ride side by side.

9

'There ain't no way they coulda not seen 'em.'

Bull Whetstine leaned against the corral, scowling at the distance. 'Three of 'em, you say?'

'Three of 'em,' Lonnie affirmed. 'They wasn't all in one spot, either. They was all in different places. There wasn't any brush that woulda kept anyone from seein' 'em, if they was lookin'. They'd all three been there long enough they was dead, an' their calves was already starved to death. Well, one of 'em starved to death. He was still layin' there. Somethin' ate the other two. But the bog was dried up enough they wouldn'ta bogged down in it for several days already. It ain't rained or nothin' up there fer two or three weeks, so the bogs is dryin' up.'

'You didn't find any fresh ones bogged down?'

'Yeah. We spotted one. She'd been in there a day or so, looked like. She still stood all right when we hauled her out. Her calf was suckin' good an everythin' when we left.'

'So what d'ya think?'

Lonnie shook his head. 'I don't guess it's my place to think. I ain't sure I'd even say anything, you knowin' there's bad blood between me an' him anyway. I'd be afraid you'd think I was just tryin' to use you to get at him.'

Bull shook his head. 'No, I know you too well for that, Lonnie. You've always been a straight shooter. I don't think you'd lie to save your skin. I meant, why do you think Arn and Wes didn't see them heifers bogged down?'

Lonnie sighed heavily. He pursed his lips. He kicked at the dirt with the toe of his boot. At last he said, 'I don't think they was even up there.'

Bull nodded. 'That's what I was thinkin', too. Of course, that don't prove they robbed that stage, though.'

'But it takes away their alibi for 'Where was they?' ' Lonnie countered.

'Yeah, but that ain't my worry,' Bull said. 'My worry is I sent a couple hands to check on cows and they didn't do it. Now we lost three head o' cows an' three calves because of it.'

'I guess that ain't my place to worry about either,' Lonnie said. 'I just thought you needed to know what me'n Corky found up there.'

'I wanta have a word with you about that, too.'

'About what?'

'You an' Corky ridin' off up there.'

'Why?'

'Well, I ain't sure it's my place, but I ain't sure it ain't. When I send you off to do a job, I expect you to do it. I don't expect you to be invitin' the boss's daughter to go with you.'

'What're you sayin', Bull?'

'I'm sayin' it don't look good. I don't know why Ira ain't clumb your frame about it, but Corky's a woman now. She ain't just the boss's kid no more. She's a right good-lookin' woman, as a matter of fact. You already let it be known you was sweet on her, when you tangled with Arn about her. Then you go ridin' off alone, just the two of you, for the whole day, and come back three hours after dark a gigglin' and chatterin' like a couple o' schoolkids; it don't look good. I ain't gonna have a hand that's workin' for me ruinin' that girl's reputation. If you wanta hang around her when you got time and you're close to the ranch, that's a different thing. But when you're ridin' off a long way thataway, I expect you to do it alone.'

Lonnie's face registered alternating anger, embarrassment and concern. When Bull finished, he said, 'I never even give a thought to how it might look.'

'I didn't think you did. I know you'd sure never want a bunch o' gossip to start about that girl.'

'No, I sure wouldn't. I'd kill a man that started any.'

116

'Well, you might have to hang yourself, then,' Bull rejoined. 'If talk starts, it'll be 'cause you an' her was off in the mountains by yourselves for that long.'

'Well, I gotta admit you're right. I'll give a thought to it next time.'

'I was sure you would. Now, if you would, I'd like for you to back me.'

'Back you doin' what?'

'I'm headin' over to the bunkhouse to can a couple liars. I ain't likely to need any help, but I'd take kindly to your bein' there just in case. They're both pretty handy with their guns.'

'You already backed Arn down once, too. You know I'll back your play. Give me a few minutes to get myself set in the bunkhouse.'

'I'll be there in about fifteen minutes.'

Lonnie hurried to finish what he was doing, then headed for the bunkhouse. Nearly a dozen hands were there, including Arn and Wes, lounging on their bunks. Lonnie walked to the small table that stood against the wall at one end of the long room. It was there that hands whiled away winter hours playing cards. He took a chair at the table, with his back to the wall. As casually as he could, he removed his gun from its holster and laid it on the table in front of him, as though he were preparing to clean it.

He hadn't more than gotten set when Bull stepped in the door. An air of expectancy rippled through the room. Most of the hands tensed visibly. Bull wasted no time.

'Arn, Wes, get your gear packed. Here's the wages you got comin', through today. I want you both off the TS Bar within the hour.'

Wes jerked erect, but Arn stood up slowly from his bunk.

'You cannin' us?'

'Consider yourselves canned,' Bull replied.

'What for?'

'Take your pick,' Bull responded. 'If a man doesn't do what he's told, I'll generally give him another chance or two. If a man lies to me, he's gone. You boys was sent to do a job, and you didn't do it. Then you lied about it, so nobody else did it either. Them heifers you was sent to check on needed checked on. You never went. Because of that, we lost three head of cows and their calves. There ain't room on this place for a liar, let alone two.'

'Who told you we never went up there?'

'The dead heifers that bogged down and died. There ain't no way they wasn't already bogged down when you was supposed to be checkin' on 'em.'

'That what pretty boy over there told you?'

Bull nodded. 'That's what I sent him up there to check on. Of course, if you want to call him a liar, you gotta do the same for the one that went with him.'

'Who's that?' Arn demanded.

'Don't know that's any o' your business. You're wastin' time. Your hour started several minutes ago. Get to pickin' up your stuff.'

Arn and Wes took turns glaring daggers at Bull, then at Lonnie. Eventually they turned to their bunks and began gathering their possessions. When they were finished, they shouldered their bed-rolls, with their possessions rolled into them, and headed out the door. Bull stood at the door and watched in silence as they went.

When they headed for the barn, Bull followed, with Lonnie staying a ways behind and to one side. Together they watched the pair saddle their horses and mount up. As they rode out of the yard, Arn said:

'You ain't seen the last of us. You'll wish a whole lotta times you never crossed us.'

'Just ride,' Bull growled.

The two spurred their horses and rode from the yard at a gallop.

Bull sighed heavily as he watched them go. 'I've canned a lot of cowboys,' he said. 'But I got a bad feeling about this. I'm afraid he just may be right. We likely ain't seen the last of them two.'

A gnawing ache in the pit of his stomach assured Lonnie that he was right.

10

'You boys got business in town?'

Arn Banning and Wes Ulger looked up from the beers they were nursing. 'Havin' a drink, Sheriff,' Arn responded. 'Ain't no law against that, is there?'

'Not if that's all you're doing,' Ike Hardy responded. 'But I been wantin' to talk to you boys.'

'Yeah? What about?'

'About that stage robbery we talked about before.'

'What about it? We already told you where we were when that happened.'

'Yeah, but your story don't check out. I talked to Whetstine yesterday. He says he canned you two boys for not bein' where you were supposed to be that day.'

'That ain't got nothin' to do with you.'

'Don't it? The day you weren't where he sent you was the same day the stage was robbed and them two men were killed. The reason you said you couldn't have done it was 'cause you was up there past Thompson Rim, checkin' them heifers. Now Bull tells me you wasn't up there at all. Where were you boys that day?'

'That ain't none o' your business,' Wes growled.

'I'll agree with that,' Arn said. 'We don't have any reason to account to you for our whereabouts.'

'You do if there's a crime involved.'

'No crime that we done,' Arn argued. 'If you got some evidence it was us, then we might have to answer for where we were and what we was doin'. But you ain't, so we don't have to tell you nothin'.'

Ike glared at the two in the frustration of knowing Arn was right. 'I'll get it,' he assured them. 'And when I do, I'll be comin' after you two.'

'Any time you think you're man

enough, you come ahead,' Arn blustered.

Ignoring the response, Ike continued, ' . . . and in the meantime, I'd take it kindly if you boys would find someplace else to hang out. We don't really need your kind hangin' around this town.'

Arn set up straight in his chair. His hand dropped to his leg, just by the butt of his pistol. 'Now, Sheriff, that ain't a kind thing to say. In fact, I don't think it's a legal thing to say either. If we ain't done nothin' that you can prove, then we ain't no different than any other cowpokes out of a job an' lookin' for work. There ain't no law against that. You got no reason to try to run us outa town, an' we ain't goin'. What are you gonna do about it?'

The muscles at the hinge of Ike's jaw bulged and flexed as he stared at the two. Once again, however, he knew they were right. He could not step outside the limits of the law, even if he knew their presence would be trouble. 'Just remember what I said,' he told them as he turned to leave.

As he stepped out of sight beyond the front door, Arn and Wes both released a huge sigh.

'I thought he was gonna try an' take us,' Wes breathed.

'Let 'im try,' Arn responded. 'He ain't half as tough as he makes out.'

Wes busied himself regathering his courage. 'Besides, he ain't got nothin' on us at all,' he iterated. 'If he did, he'd try to arrest us. There ain't no proof we was even anywhere around where that stage was robbed.'

A soft voice broke into their conversation. 'You were, though.'

Both men whirled to face the new voice. A young cowboy faced them. Something in his stance, in his eyes, in the set of his jaw spoke of age beyond his years.

'Who're you?' Arn asked.

'My name's Kyle Slaughter.'

Arn frowned. 'Name don't ring a bell to me.'

'Me neither,' Wes agreed.

'How about Ralph Slaughter? Ever hear of him?'

'Never heard of him,' Arn denied.

'Me neither,' Wes echoed.

'He was a man about five ten. On the heavy side. Good sized belly. Wore a tall hat with the crown crimped on all four sides, so it sorta came to a peak.'

Arn's face suddenly blanched, but Wes's face reflected only blank confusion.

'You look like that rung a bell,' the young man said.

'Can't say that it does,' Arn lied.

'How about if I tell you he was a passenger on that stage that was robbed?'

Realizing where the conversation was leading, other patrons of the saloon began moving away from the trio, gathering at the walls out of any likely line of fire.

'Don't know what that would have to do with us,' Arn lied again.

Wes's eyes flew open a notch wider than they were already. He shot a quick

126

glance at Arn, then back at the stranger. His face paled noticeably.

'What's that guy to you?' Wes asked.

'Strange that you should ask,' the stranger said softly. 'He was my pa. He was comin' out here to try to talk me outa my wayward ways, and get me to go back East with him.'

'You a hired gun?' Arn asked.

'I've made a livin' with my gun,' the stranger admitted, 'but this is personal. I think you boys killed my pa. And I ain't the sheriff. I don't need a lot of proof.'

Arn and Wes both stood up slowly and moved away from each other, away from the table. The young man bracing them neither moved nor changed expression.

'You think you can take us both?' Wes asked.

'If I have to,' Slaughter replied. 'The choice is yours. You can walk across the street and tell the sheriff how you held up that stage and killed those two men, or you can take your chances with me.'

'You're makin' a big mistake,' Wes insisted. 'We didn't have nothin' to do with that stage. We maybe wasn't takin' care o' business like the foreman sent us to do, but we wasn't robbin' no stage, neither.'

'We'll let the court decide that, I guess,' Slaughter responded.

'I guess not,' Arn said. His voice was light and pleasant, but his eyes were flat and totally without expression. 'If you're fixin' to do somethin', do it.'

Slaughter responded by whipping his gun from its holster. His hand was a blur of movement. In the smallest fraction of a second, his gun was clear of leather and raising to align itself on the front of Arn's shirt.

Fast as he was, he was no match for Arn. Arn's gun was in his hand spouting fire and lead before Slaughter's gun was even level. Slaughter grunted and took a step backward. He looked at the gun in Arn's hand in confusion, just as a second slug slammed into him.

Wes finally got his gun clear of its holster as the echoes of Arn's second shot died away. He watched slack-mouthed as Slaughter collapsed to a sitting position, then fell over sideways. His gun still lay in his limp hand, its hammer cocked.

'Wow! He was fast!' Wes breathed.

'Not too bad at that,' Arn agreed.

Just then the sheriff burst back in through the door.

'What's goin' on in here?'

'Just defendin' ourselves,' Arn said. His voice was calm, but his dancing eyes mocked the sheriff.

Wes holstered his guns. Arn calmly ejected the two spent casings from his own and reloaded from the cartridge belt at his waist. Then he turned the cylinder to be sure it was moving freely. Then he dropped it back into its holster. His hand stayed just by the butt of it. Ike glared at the two of them, then turned his attention to the bartender.

'What happened, Tug?'

The bartender shrugged. 'Like he

says, Sheriff. The kid said his name's Kyle Slaughter. Says his pa was killed in that stage hold-up. Accused Wes and Arn of doin' it. He forced the issue. He thought he was gunman enough to take 'em both, I guess. He wasn't.'

Frustration spread across Ike's face. He looked around the room. 'Anybody disagree with that?'

A murmur of voices affirmed the bartender's account. Ike sighed heavily. 'I'll let it go at that, then, providin' you two get out of town. I can lock you up pending an investigation, if you still think you don't need to go.'

Arn's flippant attitude changed to irritation. He started to say something, then thought better of it. At last he said, 'C'mon, Wes. This town's startin' to stink.'

'That's the rotten tail on your hat that stinks,' the sheriff argued.

Arn opened his mouth to retort, then closed it and walked out, closely followed by Wes.

11

'Did you hear what happened in town yesterday?'

'Yeah. Don't surprise me none. That Arn is greased lightning with a gun.'

'He don't never miss, neither. I seen 'im whip that gun out an' pop a runnin' cottontail in the head onct. Did it so fast I couldn't even see 'im move. One second he's just standin' there, an' his gun goes off, an' the rabbit flips up in the air an' turns a somersault an' lands on the ground, an' he's standin' there with a wisp o' smoke comin' outa his gun barrel, kinda smilin'. I never seen the like.'

'Guy he killed was a hired gunman.'

'No kiddin'? And Arn was faster?'

'Way faster. He even let the hired gun draw first, then shot him twice before he could get his gun up.'

'You don't say! Who told you?'

'Grumpy. He was in town after some stuff, an' stopped off for a beer. Saw the whole thing.'

The crew of the TS Bar were standing in a bunch, waiting their riding orders for the day. Their buzz of conversation faded down to an occasional mutter, then silence, as Bull, the foreman, walked over and stopped in front of them. His face was drawn tight.

'We won't be ridin' out today, boys.'

'What, why not? What happened?' a dozen voices at once wondered.

'The boss's ma passed on in the night,' Bull announced. 'They found her dead in her bed when she didn't get up for breakfast. Seemed to die peaceful. The bed wasn't tore up or nothin'. Heart just stopped, most likely. I already sent Curly after the preacher about three hours ago.'

'Just as well,' a cowboy said softly. 'She'd just plumb lost her mind a'ready. That ain't no way to live.'

'Yeah, that's true,' Bull agreed, 'but she was still Ira's ma. He'll grieve her just as much as if she was in the prime of life. You boys can busy yourselves with fixin' up your gear and mendin' whatever needs mendin' this mornin'. The preacher oughta be here shortly after noon. We'll have a funeral for her then. I need a couple or three of you boys to dig the grave. Then I'll be expectin' you all to warsh up an' put on your Sunday duds, to show the boss the respect and all.'

Three of the men quickly volunteered to dig the grave. Bull looked around. 'Where's Puke?'

Lonnie said, 'I dunno, Bull, but he don't look good this mornin'. He was about white as a ghost at breakfast. Didn't eat more'n half a dozen bites, then he jumped up an' left, like he was gonna go puke some more.'

'You better go check on 'im,' Bull responded.

Lonnie left the group at once, and Bull answered questions from those curious about the day's schedule or the old woman's death. He was still there when Lonnie came back, a worried expression on his face.

'You better come check Puke out, Bull.'

'He pukin' again?'

'Yeah, but not like usual.'

'What d'ya mean?'

'It's mostly blood,' Lonnie said. 'He's puked up so much blood I don't know how he's still standin'. He's just leanin' agin the back o' the bunkhouse.'

Bull hurried with Lonnie to check on the young hand. Several of the other hands followed. When they walked around the corner, Puke was just sliding down the wall to a sitting position. His face was almost totally devoid of color. His eyes were glazed.

'What's wrong, Puke?' Bull demanded, kneeling by him.

Puke looked up at the foreman, focusing his eyes with a visible effort.

'Don't feel too good today, Bull. I'll be OK, though. Just need to rest a bit.'

The words were barely out of his mouth when he turned his head and heaved. A large stream of bright red, frothy blood gushed from his mouth, spewing over the ground already covered with the gore.

Bull turned to one of the hands who'd followed them. 'Hank, grab the fastest horse you can and hightail it to town after the doc. Get 'im back here just as quick as you can.'

Hank whirled and left at a run. Bull continued: 'Lonnie, Brick, Fred, grab Puke and get 'im into the bunkhouse. Lester, get a bucket for him to puke in.'

The three men Bull had designated picked the young man up as gently as they could and hurried round the building and in the front door. They were just putting him on the bunk when Lester rushed in the door with the bucket. They got it under Puke's head just in time to catch another stream of pure blood gushing from his mouth.

They laid him back on the bed and straightened his legs. Lonnie picked up one arm that dangled over the side of the bunk, and laid it across his stomach. Puke opened his eyes. 'Don't feel very good,' he mumbled. 'I'll be all right. Just tired.'

At the end of the sentence his voice was so soft they could barely hear it. He closed his eyes. Three of the men stayed there, holding the bucket ready, talking worriedly to each other. Half an hour passed.

'He ain't puked for a while,' one of them said hopefully.

'He ain't done nothin' else, either,' another responded. 'You sure he's breathin'?'

The first speaker laid a hand on the young man's chest. He could feel no pulse, no movement. 'Better go get Bull,' he said softly.

One of the hands left, returning with the foreman less than three minutes later. Bull checked the young man over, confirming that he was dead.

'What happened?' one of those attending him asked the foreman.

Bull shrugged. 'Hard to say. Bad stomach. Had a bad stomach when I hired him. It always seemed to get worse when he was worryin' about somethin'. I 'spect it just got worse. Somethin' musta busted, an' he just plumb bled to death inside. Well, I guess you boys had just as well dig another grave. We'll get double duty outa the preacher.'

'He got family?'

'Don't know of any.'

'What's his name?'

'Don't rightly know. Puke's all I ever heard 'im called.'

It wasn't until the preacher had arrived and both bodies had been laid out beside the open graves that anyone knew any different. As the preacher began, he asked, 'And what is the young man's name?'

There was an awkward silence, until Corky spoke up. 'Sean. His name was Sean Granger.'

Everyone looked at Corky for a moment in surprise, until the preacher spoke again. 'And does the young man have any family?'

Another silence ensued, broken finally as a cowboy cleared his throat. 'He come from Missouri, but his folks is dead. He told me that once. Didn't talk much about it.'

The preacher nodded. He proceeded to conduct the funeral, then both bodies were lowered gently into the graves. The preacher intoned the words of committal. As he twice spoke the words, 'earth to earth, ashes to ashes, dust to dust,' he sprinkled handfuls of the fresh earth on to the bodies, wrapped in blankets and tightly bound. Then he stepped back and motioned. Four of the hands stepped forward and quickly filled in the graves, mounding them up as evenly as they could. The preacher then spoke words of benediction, and the small gathering began to disperse.

'Wonder who's next?' one cowboy wondered aloud.

'What d'ya mean?'

'Things always happen in threes. Two died. Wonder who's next.'

'Maybe the guy that got killed in town was the third.'

'Couldn't be. He wasn't from this outfit.'

'But the guy that killed him was.'

'Yeah, but not no more. He'd done been canned already. I don't think that'd count.'

'Maybe it won't happen in threes this time.'

'Yeah. Maybe.'

Corky sought out Lonnie. 'Are you sure Sean didn't have any folks?' she asked.

Lonnie sighed. 'I don't know. He never mentioned any. Never wrote any letters. Never got any. If he did, I guess they didn't care much about him. How'd you know his name?'

She shrugged. 'He offered to take care of my horse when I came home once. I felt funny calling him 'Puke.' That's such an awful name. So I asked him what his name really was, and he told me. After that I always called him 'Sean', instead of 'Puke', and he always grinned like I'd given him a ten dollar bill every time I did.'

'Who'd've thought it'd mean anything to 'im.' Lonnie mused. 'I wish I'da known it mattered to him.'

Corky's voice was hard, almost brittle. 'Why do men have such a hard time telling anyone what matters to them?' she asked.

'Don't wanta be weak, I guess,' he offered. 'Or a bellyacher. Nobody likes a bellyacher.'

'You don't have to be a bellyacher to say what matters to you,' she insisted.

'I s'pose not.'

'So what matters to you, Lonnie Bursell?'

Catching her totally off guard, he said, 'You do.'

'What?'

'You matter to me.'

'What do you mean?'

'Well, you said men was supposed to say what matters to 'em. So I'm just doin' what you said. I'm sayin' that most of all, more'n anything I know in this world, you matter to me. And if I up an' died all of a sudden like Puke . . . I mean, Sean did, I wouldn't want to do it without you knowin' how I feel.'

Corky felt her heart pounding in her ears. She knew her face must be brilliant red, and she didn't even care. She looked up into the earnest openness of his eyes.

'Lonnie Bursell, are you finally telling me that you love me?'

Something flashed across his face that she could not begin to understand. In its wake, he sighed heavily. He opened his mouth, and words began to pour out like a torrent.

'Little Cowgirl, I have been in love with you for the past four or five years. I dream about you. I think about you. I get so crabby nobody can stand to be around me if I go more'n two days without talkin' to you. And I always knowed you weren't noways interested in some poor dumb cowboy, and I didn't expect you to be. But then, you just said men was supposed to up and say what matters to 'em, so I am. You do. I guess I just finally got up nerve to up and say, 'I love you, Little Cowgirl.' '

'Lonnie Bursell, if you don't shut up and kiss me, I'm going to stomp on your toe. And after you do, I'll tell you how long I've been in love with you.'

He did.

She did.

And a day of death and grief on the TS Bar seemed suddenly to be the most wonderful day there ever was.

12

'The house seems so empty without Mamaw.'

Ira looked at his daughter through the cloud of smoke from his pipe. 'It does for a fact,' he agreed.

'Quiet, too,' Corky lamented.

'I certainly don't miss her bemoaning whatever she did that got her in trouble,' Theda offered.

'No, I can't say I miss that any,' Ira agreed with her as well.

'She never even said what it was,' Corky pondered.

'Prob'ly wasn't much of anything. Leastwise, I'm gonna think it wasn't much. I'spect maybe it happened when she was a little tyke.'

'They wouldn't have locked her up for something if she was just a child,' Theda argued. 'She kept saying all the time that she was locked up, and her parents had to come get her out. That sounds like more than stealing candy from the store or something.'

'Maybe she was involved in one of those suffrage marches or something,' Corky offered.

'Don't know,' Ira dismissed the subject. 'We won't ever know. So there's no sense in chewin' on it and ponderin' it and guessing. So far as I know, my mother never did anything to be that ashamed of. I'm going to think it was something she read in a book, and when her mind went bad she somehow remembered it, but by then she thought it was something that had happened to her.'

Theda studied her husband's face closely. 'Well, that's a real possibility,' she conceded. 'That makes more sense than anything else. That's probably why she never even said what it was. She hadn't really done anything.'

Corky looked back and forth between her parents several times, trying to figure out whether her mother was sincere, or if she was only trying to ease her father's mind. In the end she decided it didn't matter. She realized for the first time that her mother was a very astute woman, and loved her father with an intense loyalty.

She hid a smile as she said, 'I'm going for a ride.'

'Where you going?' Ira demanded.

'Oh, probably up toward the rim. Why?'

'I'd rather you didn't.'

'Why?'

'Just rather you didn't.'

'But, Papa! I always ride up there. I love it up there.'

'I know that. Everyone else knows that, too.'

'What's that supposed to mean?'

Ira took a deep breath. 'Little Filly, there's a couple of men runnin' around the country that are about as bad a pair as I've run across. One of 'em is known to have a hankerin' for you. And he knows as well as I do how much you like to ride up by the rim.

As long as they're runnin' loose around the country, I want you to stick close to the place, or take somebody with you.'

'Can Lonnie go with me?'

'I ain't sure that's such a good idea either. I seen the way you two been hangin' all over each other the past week or two.'

Corky giggled. 'Well, at least you know he'll look out for me.'

'Yeah, but who's going to go along to keep him in line?'

Corky giggled again. Theda said, 'Ira! Stop that! You talk like Coralee's one of those easy girls or something.'

'No, I ain't sayin' that,' Ira argued. 'But I know what it's like bein' young and in love. Don't tell me you've forgot all the ways we had of sneakin' away by ourselves.'

'Ira!' Theda protested.

'You didn't!' Corky exulted. 'Tell me about it.'

Theda's face turned so brilliantly red her ears seemed to glow. 'You just mind your own business, Coralee,' she scolded.

'Somebody comin',' Ira interrupted.

The three walked together to the front door and out onto the porch. 'Buckboard comin',' Ira announced.

'Who is it, Papa?'

'Can't tell yet. It should be Curly. He took the buckboard to town yesterday for a bunch of supplies. Don't look like him drivin' it, though. Looks like maybe Ike.'

'Why would he be bringing our buckboard home?'

'We'll know in a minute.'

By the time Sheriff Hardy reined the buckboard into the yard, half a dozen hands were ranged around the yard watching.

'Body in the back, with the rest of the stuff,' somebody announced.

A pall of silence descended on the yard. In that silence, the blowing and stamping of the team seemed inordinately loud. The squeaking of the seat as Ike Hardy climbed down even seemed to echo in the yard.

'Evenin', Ira. Theda. Miss Stern-hagen.'

'Evenin', Sheriff,' Ira responded for them. 'What you got?'

'One of your crew, I'm afraid.'

'Who?'

'Curly Winfield.'

Ira's jaw bunched tightly. Corky saw his hand clench and unclench at his side several times before he answered. 'Bull sent him to town yesterday. Supposed to be back tonight. What happened?'

The sheriff sighed. 'I ain't rightly sure. I get a little different story from everybody. The only things I'm real sure about is he run into Arn and Wes.'

'Them two again!'

The sheriff nodded. 'They was baitin' 'im pretty hard, it sounds like. He was mostly ignorin' 'em, puttin' together the supplies. He was about loaded an' ready to go. Then Arn went an' said somethin' that set 'im off. He tried to draw on 'em.'

'He tried to draw against Arn and Wes both?'

'Yup. Every witness I questioned all said that Curly drew first. Arn stood there and waited till Curly's gun was clear outa the holster, then he pulled his gun and shot him before Curly could even pull the trigger. Wes got into the act, too, but it was Arn that got 'im first. They musta put six or eight slugs into 'im.'

'Why would Curly do somethin' that dumb? What did they say to 'im?'

'Well,' the sheriff hesitated, 'I ain't sure that anybody actually heard everything that was said, just exactly.'

'But you do know what it was,' Ira insisted.

The sheriff hesitated again. 'Well, the gist of it anyway.'

'And?' Ira insisted again.

The sheriff hesitated another long moment before he said, 'Arn said something about your daughter. About him and your daughter.'

Corky gasped and put her hands to

her mouth. Ira's mouth tightened to an almost seamless line. Theda's face turned red in anger, rather than embarrassment.

'How dare he!' Theda said.

'Why, that, that . . . ' Corky sputtered.

Ira's voice was quiet. Something in it sent shivers up and down Corky's spine. 'He has said some things about her before,' he confirmed. 'In fact, Lonnie beat him like a rug on a clothesline for it, once.'

The sheriff's eyebrows shot up. 'And lived to tell about it? I wondered where he got worked over, an' who by. Some of the marks still show on his face. Your man did a good job of it. How did it happen that he didn't get shot for it?'

'It happened that Bull was pointin' a shotgun at his middle when it came to that,' Ira explained. 'Even Arn ain't good enough to go against a Greener, when Bull Whetstine's pointin' it at 'im.'

'Then Bull and Lonnie had best both watch their backs,' Ike declared.

'They are,' Ira confirmed. 'Looks like they're trying to get us mad enough to come after 'em.'

'Could be. I'll be needin' your word that you won't, though.'

'Why?'

'Why do I need your word, or Why are you not going to?'

'Why wouldn't we go after 'em?'

'Because it's against the law. The same reason I couldn't arrest them for it. Curly drew first. That made it self-defense, even if they did egg it on.'

'It's murder, any way you look at it,' Ira argued.

'Not the way the law looks at it,' Ike insisted. 'And we got to go by the law, even when it sits in the center of our gut like a hot rock to do it.'

Ira glared at the lawman. At last he said, 'You'll be needin' a bait o' grub afore you head back for town?'

Not knowing if he had won the argument or not, Ike knew it would be futile to argue it further. 'I'd appreciate it,' he said.

'One of you boys tell Cookie to rustle up a bait o' grub for the sheriff.'

'Much obliged,' Ike said. He turned and walked to the cookhouse.

The rest of the crew began to organize for another burial. 'You want me to ride after the preacher?' somebody asked.

Ira shook his head. 'Curly was never a religious sort. I'll say a few words over him when you're ready.'

It was dark by the time they had finished. The crew dispersed after the fresh earth was mounded over the dead cowboy.

'I told you things happen in threes.'

'Yeah. I hope that's the end of it.'

'Not likely.'

'What do you mean?'

'As long as them two's runnin' around the country, folks is gonna keep gettin' kilt.'

'They're a bad pair, all right.'

'Not Wes. He's just an idiot. Hangs

on to Arn 'cause he thinks it makes him somebody.'

'Gonna make him a dead somebody.'

'More'n likely. I don't care, as long as Arn goes with him.'

'Sure like to get my hands on 'im.'

'Not me. I sure hope somebody gets their hands on 'im that can handle him.'

Nobody among the crew thought they had seen or heard the last of the pair.

13

'Cloud o' dust comin'.'

There were only half a dozen of the TS Bar hands in and around the ranch yard. Grumpy Wollesen, the aging flunkee, first spotted the approach and called out to whomever was within hearing.

Every hand stopped what they were doing and drifted to the yard, watching the approaching dust. Some mystic force seemed to convey an air of expectant dread that permeated the crew.

'Sure in a hurry,' one of them commented.

'Gonna ride their horses plumb into the ground,' Grumpy agreed. 'Then they're gonna want fresh horses, and they'll take off agin on a dead run. Then they're gonna say, 'Grumpy, you get all these horses rubbed down an' cooled off an' give 'em some oats.' And if any of 'em dies from bein' run to death, or comes up lame, or drinks too much an' founders, you know who they're gonna blame for it. 'Grumpy, why didn't you take better care o' them horses?' they'll ask me. Ride 'em in fallin' down ready to die, an' expect me to make 'em all fine, sure's anything.'

'Must be half a dozen at least,' another observed.

'Oh, sure,' Grumpy agreed. 'Prob'ly eight or ten. More horses for old Grumpy to take care of that way. Wonder what they'd do if they had the rheumatism like I got. Sit in their rockin' chair and moan an' whine about it, most as like.'

'It's the sheriff,' someone announced. 'Seen the sun shine off'n his badge.'

'Looks like a posse.'

'What d'ya bet it's got somethin' to do with Arn and Wes.'

'Wouldn't be surprised. Maybe they kilt the wrong fella this time.'

The dust cloud began to take form,

as six riders became visible at the leading edge of it. Ira stepped into the yard to await their arrival. Theda and Corky stood just outside the door on the porch, waiting and watching as well.

The posse thundered into the yard, hauling their horses to a stop in a flurry of dust.

'You're in a big hurry,' Ira observed.

'How many hands you got handy?' Ike Hardy asked, without any of the customary preliminaries.

Ira frowned. 'Well, what you see, right here. Bull and four of the boys are less than a mile off, most likely. They're gatherin' bulls, gettin' ready to take 'em up an' turn 'em in with the cows. I can send someone to have 'em here in half an hour or so. What's going on?'

'Well, they went and done it, this time.'

'Who? Done what?'

'Them two finally stepped over the line.'

Ira turned to one of the hands that was standing, listening, 'Frank, why don't you saddle up and go fetch Bull and the boys with him. Tell 'im they're needed here.'

As the cowhand turned to comply, Ira turned his attention back to the sheriff. 'Now how about you slow down and fill me in on what you're talkin' about,' he suggested.

The sheriff took a deep breath. He lifted his right foot out of the stirrup and hooked it around the saddle horn in front of him. He reached into his pocket and fished out a bag of tobacco and a package of papers. He said nothing as he shook out the tobacco into the paper he held cupped with his other hand. He took the drawstring in his teeth, pulled the sack of tobacco closed and dropped it back in his pocket. Then he used both hands to carefully roll the paper around the tobacco, twisting one end tightly. He put the untwisted end in his mouth and fished a match out of his pocket. He struck the match on the pommel of his saddle, shielding it with both hands from the light breeze. He lit the cigarette and sucked in a big breath of its smoke. He exhaled it slowly, then spoke.

'The store in town got robbed last night.'

'That so?'

The sheriff nodded. 'They killed old Herm Westfield.'

'You don't say!'

The sheriff nodded again. 'Shot 'im down in cold blood, looks like. Herm didn't even have a gun on 'im, so it couldn'ta been self-defense this time.'

'Who done it?'

'Well, nobody saw it. Some heard the shots, though. Saw two men run outa the store an' run around back. Then they heard their horses take off a-runnin'.'

'They get a good look at 'em?'

'Nobody seen their faces, but they got a good enough look, all right.'

'How'd they get a good enough look if they didn't see their faces?'

'Seen their hats.'

Ira stared at the sheriff in total incomprehension, but he waited in silence while Ike took another long drag from the cigarette. Then he explained. 'One of the hats had a big ol' squirrel tail danglin' from the back of the hatband.'

'Arn,' Ira breathed.

The sheriff nodded. 'Couldn'ta been nobody else. The other man answered Wes's description just fine.'

'If that was last night, how come you're just now gettin' out here? Did they come this way?'

The sheriff nodded. 'They was headed this way, looked like, but it was pertneart dark already, and no way we could follow them in the dark. We waited till daybreak, an' started trackin' 'em. Roan Eagle was in town, so I went an' hired him to track 'em for us.'

'You trackin' 'em on a dead run? Even Roan Eagle ain't that good.'

The sheriff shook his head. 'We tracked 'em a good ways, until we seen where they was headin'. They're headin' for Grady's Hole, up in the mountains, looks like. Once they get up there, it'll take more'n half a dozen guys to smoke 'em out. That's when I decided we'd sidetrack an' ride over here. Bull knows that country like the back of his hand. Once we figure out where they're holed up, he kin tell us how to work in on 'em. I wanta throw down on 'em when they ain't got no chance o' shootin' up my posse.'

'Makes sense,' Ira conceded. 'Well, you'd all just as well get down an' walk your horses around a bit. Get 'em cooled down. You can give 'em a bait o' grain in the barn. By the time you get them taken care of, Cookie'll have some grub ready for you. Bull an' the boys will be here by then, and we'll set out.'

'You'll be comin' too?'

'Wouldn't miss it. I owe those two. They killed one o' my hands. They lied about my girl and sullied her reputation. It's time somebody put an end to them two.'

An hour and a half later the posse,

doubled in size now, rode out of the yard provisioned for as long as it took to ride the pair to ground. As they were getting ready to mount up, Lonnie spotted Corky, standing at the corner of the house. He glanced around quickly, then walked over to her.

'Honey, be careful,' Corky said.

Lonnie felt himself cringe at the fear in her voice. 'We ain't gonna take any chances,' he assured her. 'That's why we got such a big posse.'

'But I've seen Arn shoot. He's really, really good.'

'Yeah, well, every man in this posse can do a pretty good job o' that, too.'

'Not like Arn,' she protested. 'I watched him draw and shoot those two squirrels before even they could move. And squirrels are really quick.'

'Don't worry yourself about it,' Lonnie tried to reassure her. 'We'll be careful.'

'But he'll kill you first, if he gets a chance. And if anything happened to you, I, I don't think I could stand that. I love you.'

'Hey, don't worry so much. I'll be fine.'

'Promise me you'll be careful.'

'OK. I promise.'

'And kiss me 'bye.'

'Right out here in front o' God an' everybody.'

'Right out here in front of God and Papa and everybody,' she smirked.

He did, and suddenly wished he didn't have to go anywhere. At least they both knew he'd hurry back.

The sheriff led the way back to where they had broken off the trail to ride to the ranch. This time they rode at a brisk trot, saving the horses.

When they got back to the trail the fleeing pair had left, Roan Eagle resumed his place at the lead. The trail was plain enough for him to continue the brisk trot.

'Sure don't know what he's seein',' somebody commented.

'Seems sure of hisself.'

'Them Injuns kin see a trail where

there ain't none.'

'I swear, Roan Eagle kin track a butterfly, just by the wind from its wings movin' the grass.'

Lonnie chuckled at the comments, but he was as impressed as the rest with the Indian's ability to see the trail. He could catch a glimpse occasionally of a track, or some bent grass, to assure him that Roan Eagle was, in fact, following the trail. He could not have followed it, however, even at half the pace they were traveling.

Night caught them well into the mountains. As the light began to fade, Ike waved toward a spring trickling out of the rocks.

'We'll camp here. Pick up the trail at first light,' he announced.

The members of the posse unsaddled their horses and hobbled them, allowing them access to both grass and water. One of the group started laying out things to prepare a meal for them all.

'Good thinkin', bringin' George along,'

somebody complimented the sheriff.

Ike grunted. 'I been on posses afore. Good grub makes all the difference in stayin' on a trail till we catch 'em. George is worth half a dozen of you, for keepin' the rest of us in fightin' form.'

Within an hour George was hauling a pair of dutch ovens out of the coals and lifting the lids. The smell of fresh biscuits drew the members of the posse like a magnet.

To the biscuits was added meat and potatoes, fried together in three large skillets. Coffee boiled in a pair of large coffee-pots. Even Ira marveled that all that food and those cooking utensils had been packed away behind the saddles and in the saddle-bags of the men.

Lonnie wasn't sure when he'd eaten a meal on the trail as good as that one. If not for the purpose of their being there, it would have been a wonderful interlude to the demanding work. The weather was perfect. They were high enough to be above most of the bugs that so often annoyed in summertime. The scenery was beautiful. The night sky was a solid mass of twinkling stars. The soft babbling of the tiny brook was the perfect lullaby. He went to sleep with a full stomach, a full heart, and no hint of the terror that would soon overwhelm him.

14

'We got 'em!'

Sheriff Ike Hardy lifted his eyebrows questioningly. Bull Whetstine smiled tightly. 'If Roan Eagle's right, an' I 'spect he is. He's the best tracker I know. We got 'em dead to rights. That's a box canyon they're ridin' into.'

'No way out?'

'None that I know of, and I been in there a half a dozen times, gatherin' up strays.'

The posse searching for Arn and Wes sat their saddles, watching the rocks and ridges around them uneasily. Ira and Lonnie flanked Bull, watching the sheriff.

'Well, what's the plan, Ike?' Ira asked.

Ike studied the situation carefully, then turned to Bull again. 'How big's the canyon inside?'

Bull pursed his lips. 'Oh, it widens

out purty good. I'd say a good forty acres or so. The sides slope up gentle for quite a ways, then, afore it ends in cliffs an' such. Quite a bit o' timber an' brush. It's got a lot of cover. We'll have to work it slow an' careful. Make sure they can't slip past us.'

'You're sure there's no other way out?'

'Not that I know of. Oh, I'm sure a man could climb out afoot, an' I never worked the whole way around it actually lookin' fer a way out. But I never seen no tracks that any cows went out or come in any way but this here.'

Ike nodded. 'Okay. Willis and Hank, you two stay here along either side o' the way in an' out. Get yourselves set up in the rocks on either side, where you can cover it all with your rifles. Hobble your horses off yonder there, where they kin eat an' be out o' sight. Make sure neither one o' them boys gets past us an' lights outa here. The rest of you, we'll get inside where it starts widenin' out, an' we spread out in a straight line across it. We'll move forward slow an' careful. Keep your eyes peeled. Listen for sounds. Make sure you kin see the man on either side of you, so nobody can slip between you. We should be enough to make a solid line an' sweep right on through the canyon till we find 'em.'

'What do you want us to do when we spot 'em?' one of the posse asked. 'We shootin' on sight?'

Ike shook his head. 'Only if they open it up. Holler at 'em to throw down their guns. Tell 'em we got twenty men here an' they're boxed in. We'll do it by the law. I want 'em arrested an' took back to town fer a trial.'

'If they shoot?'

'Then you gotta shoot back. If they open it up, shoot to kill. They're as dangerous a pair as I've seen. Don't hold back if the shootin' starts.'

'There ain't twenty of us,' Lonnie protested.

'They don't know that,' Ike responded.

'There's enough. Let's get it done.'

Every man in the posse pulled his rifle from the saddle scabbard and levered it, to be sure a shell was ready in the chamber. Then, holding the rifles across the pommels of their saddles, they began to move slowly forward.

Thirty yards from where they had stopped to lay out the plan, the talus slopes of the narrow defile began to widen out and open up. Stretched before them a verdant expanse of grass and brush, with a few clumps of trees came into view.

'Pretty canyon,' Lonnie breathed.

'Cows like it,' Bull responded. 'There's a little spring an' a pool o' water right in the middle. Don't know where the water goes. It don't run out nowheres. Just runs into that pool.'

'Prob'ly some rock fissure it drains into if it gets too full,' Ira proposed.

'Most likely,' Bull agreed. 'I'm bettin' they'll be camped alongside that spring. There's some rocks that jut up there, an they're purty brushy. If they've heard us comin' they'll be hid in them rocks.'

'Their horses will have heard us, even if they haven't,' Lonnie observed.

The line formed across the small hidden valley. The sheriff waved his arm, and the line began moving forward. Every eye darted back and forth in front of them. Occasionally one or another would look up and survey the rocks around the rim, just in case they were riding into a trap. There was no sound other than the squeaking of their saddles and, once in a while, a horse blowing or striking a rock with its hoof.

They were approaching the center of the canyon when Bull spoke softly. 'Spring just ahead, Sheriff. Most likely spot.'

'Watch close,' the sheriff passed quietly on to the man next to him. The message passed along both ways along the advancing line.

The spring and pool of water came into the view of four of the posse, near the center of the line. Ashes of a fire made a black smear amid the green grass.

'They been here,' Lonnie breathed.

Fingers tightened on rifles. Several rifles were lifted from the saddle and held in a more nearly ready position. The horses moved steadily forward. When they were nearly to the quiet pool, Ike spoke softly. 'Two or three o' you boys dismount an' check out them rocks. We'll try to keep you covered.'

Lonnie and Ira were the first two off their horses. One of the townsmen joined them. Leaving their rifles on their horses, they drew their pistols and moved forward slowly. Keeping as low as they could, they darted to the edge of the rocks. They moved into them, climbing warily. There was nothing.

When they reached the top of the outcropping, they looked around uneasily. They could see from that vantage point the whole area in the center of the hidden glen. Nothing moved. They holstered their weapons and climbed back down.

'Nothin' there,' they reported to the sheriff.

Ike chewed his mustache thoughtfully. 'Well, they musta heard us comin' an' beat it on over to the rocks at the end. Let's keep movin'.'

They resumed the slow march of the line of nervous hunters. A deer broke from a clump of brush and bounded away, with five rifles trained on it.

'Oh, man! That scared the liver outa me!' one man exclaimed.

'Didn't do my heart a bit o' good,' another agreed.

All along the line men relaxed, relieved that it had only been a deer. 'Keep alert!' the sheriff reprimanded them. 'We're gettin' close.'

Guardedly they moved forward again. Every man felt a tight knot in the pit of his stomach. Lonnie caught himself forgetting to breathe, and scolded himself silently.

'There's the end,' Bull said softly.

'Not much place to hide, though. It just slopes up to the base o' the cliff at this end.'

Within minutes the others saw that he was right. The carpet of grass, with only occasional small clumps of brush now, sloped up the bottom of a sheer cliff. The granite wall rose more than fifty feet straight up. The line stopped, staring in confusion and disappointment.

Galloping hoofbeats approaching from behind caused every man in the posse to start and whirl, rifles coming to the ready. Roan Eagle, riding at a gallop, approached the sheriff.

Without preliminaries, sliding to a stop before the sheriff, he said, 'Them gone.'

'Whatd'ya mean, gone?' Ike demanded. 'Gone where?'

Roan Eagle pointed. 'Over there. Narrow spot. Steep climb. They go out.'

'There's another way out?' Bull demanded.

The Indian nodded. 'I ride along

edge, at end of line. See tracks. Follow. They ride out. Not here.'

'How long ago?'

'One day.'

'Well what d'ya know?' Ike marveled. 'They holed up here for one night. Made camp. Knew we couldn't get on their trail that quick. Then they lit out a way they didn't figger we'd know, an' let us spend all this time lookin' for 'em in here.'

'We follow?' Roan Eagle asked.

'Can we follow 'em?' Ike asked.

The Indian nodded. 'Slower now. Too many rocks. Roan Eagle follow trail though. I lead.'

Ike frowned. 'Seems the only choice. Somebody ride back and get Willis and Hank. We'll wait for 'em here. Just as well water your horses an' chew on whatever you got in your saddlebags to lunch on. Then we'll get movin' again.'

Lonnie said, 'I'll go get 'em,' and turned his horse back toward the entrance to the canyon. He spurred his horse to a brisk trot. As he approached the defile that gave entrance to the canyon, he called out, 'Hank! Willis! It's me, Lonnie. Don't go shootin' me.'

Both Willis and Hank stood up from behind the rocks they had taken shelter behind.

'You get 'em?' Willis called.

'No! There's another way out nobody knew about. Roan Eagle tracked 'em. They rode out yesterday. Get your horses. They're waitin' for us at the spring. We'll head out an' start trackin' 'em again.'

Grumbling and swearing, Willis and Hank climbed from the rocks and went to retrieve their horses. Lonnie lifted his right leg and hooked it around the saddle horn. He pushed his hat to the back of his head. He chewed on his upper lip.

'Why would they do that?' he asked his horse, for lack of better company. 'Why would they leave that good a trail all the way into this canyon, then sneak out the back side. They must've known there was a back way out, or they wouldn't have come here. They sure knew Ike would get Roan Eagle to track 'em. He hangs out in town enough, and everybody always talks about what a tracker he is.'

Willis and Hank approached, riding at a trot. They started to ride on by Lonnie, then stopped when it was apparent he wasn't moving. 'What're you waitin' for?' Hank asked.

Lonnie shook his head. 'Just tryin' to make sense of it,' he said. 'They left a trail all the way here, like they weren't even tryin' to hide it. They camped there beside the spring, right out in the open, like they had it figured how long it'd take us to get here, and knew they had plenty o' time. Then they did a whole lot better job o' not leavin' a trail when they snuck out the back way. It's almost like they was just baitin' us to come here an' spend a whole day or so tryin' to find 'em in the trees an' rocks o' this canyon, and never figurin' out where they went. If Roan Eagle hadn't chanced to be at the right spot to notice a track or two they did leave, we'd never know where they went.'

'Purty cagey all right,' Willis agreed. 'But why would they do that?'

'I don't know,' Lonnie conceded. 'It just don't make sense. Wish I could ask Corky. She's got a real good head for figurin' out stuff like that.'

Unbidden, his mind strayed to Corky. He thought of her face. He remembered the taste of her lips when she kissed him goodbye. He remembered her words of caution and fear for his safety. He sighed, trying to force his mind back to the business of the day.

Suddenly his eyes opened wide. Corky! She's at the ranch! With the clarity of sudden terror, he saw the whole parade of events as a cleverly arranged plot to get him and most of the rest of the hands away from the TS Bar. The whole thing was just to leave Corky unprotected. He was after Corky!

'You go with the others,' he barked. 'I got a hunch they're headin' back for the ranch. Arn's had a thing for Corky an' she brushed 'im off. Ten to one he's goin' after her.'

Without waiting for an answer he jammed the spurs into his horse's sides. The big gelding jumped with surprise and pain, and leaped forward. In four strides the gelding and Lonnie were running flat out, through the defile and into the open.

Lonnie leaned forward across the saddle horn. The front of his hat-brim blew up against the crown of his hat and stayed there. His teeth were clamped tightly. He didn't even hear the groans that squeezed through those clenched teeth with every breath.

After half a mile he reined his horse in to an easy lope. 'Better take it a little easy on you, or you won't last to the ranch,' he scolded himself.

The awful knot in his belly told him it really didn't matter. He knew he was already too late.

15

'I can't stand sitting around here!'

Theda looked up from snapping beans from the garden. 'Then you can help me get the rest of these beans snapped.'

'But we're almost done.'

'Well, then we'll find something else to work on.'

Corky lifted her hands in frustration. 'That's just it, Mama. We're just finding work to do, to stay busy. Just to stay busy. Just so we won't worry. And so all we do is stay busy, and worry anyway.'

Theda was philosophical. 'Well, there's nothing we can do about it, so we had just as well deal with it that way.'

'I don't want to deal with it that way!'

'So, do you have any better ideas?'

'Yes! I want to saddle Chico and go for a ride.'

'But you already know that isn't a good idea. Arn and Wes are out there somewhere.'

'But they're not here! They're off the other direction. You heard where Roan Eagle had tracked them. Now the whole posse is on their heels, chasing them who knows where. They're sure not going to be around here anywhere.'

'But it still makes sense for you to stay around the ranch while they're gone.'

'But the rest of the hands are trying to do all the work. I could at least ride up . . . I mean ride out and check on some of the stock.'

'Like maybe, up by Thompson Rim?'

Corky's breath escaped in a rush. 'Oh, Mama. How come you always know what I'm thinking?'

'You really like it up there, don't you?'

'I love it up there! It is so beautiful, and peaceful. There's everything there to make it the most perfect place on earth. It's warm in the sun. It's cool in the timber. There are birds and squirrels and eagles and deer and elk and rabbits and badgers and, oh, all kinds of animals. I've even seen a cougar up there a couple times.'

'Cougars are dangerous, dear.'

'Oh, not really. Not unless they're really hungry, and there are so many deer and rabbits and everything that are easy food for them, I'm not afraid of them. Besides, I could shoot one if I had to.'

Theda sighed. 'Sometime you're going to be too self-reliant for your own good.'

Corky ignored the comment. 'Besides, when I'm sitting here I'm too worried. I couldn't stand it if something happened to Lonnie.'

'You really love him, don't you?'

'Yes. I do, Mama.'

'Has he asked you to marry him?'

Corky hesitated. 'No. Not really. I mean, he sort of hinted around about it a time or two.'

'What sort of hinting?'

'Well, just asking things like what I wanted to do with my life, whether I wanted a lot of kids, things like that.'

'Oh. I see. And what did you tell him?'

'Nothing, really. Why?'

'Didn't you understand what he was doing?'

'Doing? What do you mean, Mama?'

Theda quit snapping beans and put her hands in her lap. She smiled at her daughter. 'Let me tell you something about men, dear. Then you'll understand. Men are very timid creatures. Oh, not with other men, or with horses, or things. With those things, they just use their strength and their courage and just do what they think they have to do. But with women, especially women they care about, they're very timid.'

'Afraid to talk, you mean?'

'Well, yes. That's part of it. But they're really afraid of . . . of . . . being

182

refused. You know, rejected. A man is terrified of even telling a woman he loves her, unless she tells him that she loves him first.'

'Why?'

'Because he's a man, and men are very timid that way. If Lonnie told you he loved you, and you laughed at him, or if it made you angry or afraid, or if you told him that you loved him like a brother or something, it would destroy his image of himself as a man. By saying he loved you, he would be offering himself, and you would be refusing him. Men can't deal with that very well.'

Corky smiled, as though she were suddenly invited in with her mother on some great conspiracy. 'So that's why he never told me how he felt! He just kept hinting around, until I let him know I really cared about him.'

'Exactly. And it took you long enough. He's been dropping those hints for two years or more.'

Corky's eyebrows shot up. 'He has?'

Theda chuckled. 'And you didn't even notice.'

'How do you know that?'

'Oh, I've heard him say things to you, that you thought were just casual conversation. I heard what was in his voice. You just weren't ready for that yet, and you didn't even notice.'

Corky giggled. 'He must have been so frustrated!'

'He was. But he persisted. He's had his eye on you for a very long time, you know.'

'That's why he was so mad and grumpy when Arn was flirting with me all the time.'

'Of course.'

'So what's this about his hinting around about marriage?'

'It's just more of the same thing,' Theda explained. 'The very worst thing that men are afraid of is proposing to a girl and being turned down.'

'Really?'

'Absolutely. There is no way a man offers himself to a woman any more completely than asking her to marry him. He's asking you to choose him over every other man on earth. He's asking you to give yourself to him, for your whole lifetime. And if you turn him down, it would completely destroy his ... his manhood, in his own eyes.'

'Then how does ... ? How did Papa propose to you?'

'The same way Lonnie will propose to you, I suspect. When I figured out that was what your father had in mind, I managed to let him know that I would say yes if he proposed.'

'You told him you'd say yes, even before he asked?'

'Well, not in so many words. But yes, I did. I had to. He would never have asked, if I hadn't let him know what my answer was going to be. The risk was just too great. Why, I've known a couple people that courted for ten or fifteen years, because she would never let him know that she was ready to say yes, and he just couldn't ask until he knew what

185

the answer was going to be.'

'Oh, Mama, that's just too silly. Why can't a man just ask?'

'Because men are too timid, dear, when it comes to things like that. It's just too great a risk. And that's what your Lonnie was doing, don't you see? He keeps bringing up the subject of marriage and children and things like that, just to give you a chance to let him know you're ready for him to ask you to marry him. If you let him know that you're ready, that you'll say 'yes', I bet he'll propose so fast he'll make your head swim.'

Corky chewed her lower lip, smiling, with a distant look in her eye. 'Oh, Mama! That's so funny. I think I'll just keep him wondering.'

'That's not a good idea, dear.'

'Why not?'

'It's just not a good idea to play games with your man's heart, just because you can. Things like that are a man's weakness. If you play games with his weaknesses, then you give him the right to play games with your weaknesses, too. It's awfully easy for that to turn into a game of trying to hurt each other, instead of tease each other.'

Corky grew suddenly serious. 'You mean like Henry and Maude?'

Theda nodded sadly. 'Exactly like Henry and Maude,' she agreed. 'They've spent the last twenty years learning how to hurt each other. I've never seen two more miserable people. And they love each other too much to do without each other. They just have such a habit of hurting each other they can't seem to stop.'

'So what should I do?'

'I can't tell you that, dear. But however you decide to do it, I would suggest that you let that man know you're just waiting for him to ask you, so you can say, 'yes'. He's an awfully good man, Coralee. Don't let him get away.'

'Oh, Mama, I can't wait for him to get back.'

She got up and paced around the kitchen, lost in thought. As she paced, she grew increasingly agitated. Finally she said, 'I can't just sit here and wait. I have to go for a ride, or I'm going to go crazy.'

Theda opened her mouth twice to protest, then closed it again. 'Do be careful,' she said finally.

'I will,' Corky promised. 'I'll just ride up to the rim and watch the eagles and things.'

'Be back before dark.'

Corky offered some syllable of agreement as she flew out the door. Fifteen minutes later she was loping out of the yard on Chico, the Appaloosa gelding.

Two hundred yards out of the ranch yard the gelding slowed to a swift trot. Riding easily, letting her legs absorb the jar of the horse's trot, she breathed in the clear mountain air deeply. She sighed, smiling, lost in a world of her own thoughts and dreams.

Had she been less absorbed in

thoughts of her man, she might have noticed the other two men paralleling her path, behind and a quarter mile to one side.

16

Thompson Rim loomed against the clear deep blue of the Wyoming sky. Although she knew almost every detail of the rim, Corky let her eyes drift slowly along its length, refreshing every memory.

A movement to her right caught her eye, and she turned her head to focus on the spot. A cottontail rabbit hopped out of a heavy growth of brush, and sat in the full rays of the sun, soaking up its warmth. It sat very still. Its ears were up. Its only movement was the constant twitching of its nose. Corky sat on the ground, very still, scarcely breathing, lest the rabbit catch a glimpse of movement and be frightened away.

After several minutes, the small animal hopped forward three hops and began nibbling on the leaves of a green plant. It would take a small bite, then chew very rapidly. She resisted the urge to giggle as she watched the impossibly rapid movement of the animal's jaw as it chewed.

Suddenly the rabbit's ears lay back against its head and it shot sideways into the cover of the dense brush. She heard it scurrying through the brush to safety.

She frowned, listening for whatever it may have heard.

'Sure is a nice day, ain't it?'

She started violently at the voice. She gasped and leaped to her feet. Arn Banning stood just behind where she had been sitting, grinning past a pine-needle that jutted from the corner of his mouth.

'Oh!' was all she said.

Arn's grin did not falter. 'S'prised to see me?'

Corky frantically tried to marshal her thoughts, to think, to appear less frightened than she felt. 'Arn! You startled me. I didn't hear you ride up.'

As she talked, her eyes cast wildly

about. Twenty yards to one side, Wes Ulger stood, also grinning. In his hands were the reins of his and Arn's horses, and her own Chico's as well.

'You don't watch too good when you go ridin', do you?' he teased.

'What do you mean?'

'Oh, we been followin' you ever since you left the house.'

'You . . . you've . . . you've been what?'

'Followin' you.'

'Following me? Why?'

His eyes traveled down her body and back up, stopping for what seemed like minutes on the front of her blouse. She felt herself turn crimson, feeling suddenly naked before his probing eyes. She unconsciously put a hand to the front of her blouse.

He smiled easily. 'Well now, why do you think, pretty lady. I already tol' you, I'm just plumb smitten with you. You've got to be the prettiest thing I've laid eyes on in my whole life. I been plumb pinin' away wishin' for you. That's why it upset me so much when Bull went an' canned me. Took away my excuse to stay close to you.'

'But . . . but . . . they said you .. you robbed the store in town.'

He shrugged. 'Not a bad plan, huh?'

'Plan? What do you mean?'

He reached out and traced down the side of her face with the back of a finger.

'Things has been gettin' sorta hot for me'n Wes around here. Got to seemin' like it'd be best if we just rode outa the country. I just couldn't stand the thought of leavin' here without you. You wouldn't believe how much I dream about you.'

She fought the urge to shudder at his touch. She suddenly remembered with shame how much that same touch had excited her. But it was different now. She knew what he was. She knew who she was in love with. She felt only fear and loathing at his touch now.

'That's silly,' she said.

His eyes hardened at her words, but

he showed no other effect of them. 'So I just had to have a plan,' he said softly.

'Plan?' she repeated, knowing it sounded stupid to keep saying the same thing.

He nodded. 'Sure. I couldn't just ride out here and ask you to ride off with me, even if I knew you really wanted to. If that pretty boy of yours didn't take a pot-shot at me, Bull and that shotgun o' his would. Or your pa. He's hell on wheels when he gets mad, I hear.'

'Papa?' she said, trying desperately to calm the frantic floundering of her mind.

'So me'n Wes just figured out a plan,' he boasted. 'We waited till Roan Eagle was in town. Then when it was a couple or three hours till dark, we went an' held up the store. Didn't get a whole lot o' money, but that didn't matter too much. Actually, there was quite a bit. That ain't important, though. We can always get more money. I knew if we shot old Herm, they'd get up a posse, hire Roan Eagle to track us, and come troopin' out after us.'

'You . . . you wanted them to chase you?'

'Sure? You know that box canyon up toward Gray's Hole?'

She nodded, not trusting herself to speak.

'I was hangin' around up there a couple years ago, an' found a back way outa there. Real rocky, so it wouldn't leave no trail. I had it figured to ride up there. Leave enough of a trail Roan Eagle wouldn't have no trouble findin' it. When they figured out where we went, they'd naturally ride to your place. That's the closest ranch. They'd know Bull knows the country real well. They'd just naturally take the whole crew and go troopin' up there to corner us in that box canyon. Probably creep in on foot, with twenty or thirty men, and take at least half a day doin' it. Then, when they finally reach the other end, there won't be nothin' there at all. They won't have any idea in the world where we disappeared to. They'll

195

wander around up there in the rocks for a week lookin' for us. That way, they're all gone from the ranch, and I can ride back there to get you, and we can ride outa the country together, just like I planned. Now, how's that for a good plan?'

Corky's mind whirled. 'You sneaked out of the canyon and rode back to my place?'

'Sure! That's where you were.'

'And you've been there, watching the ranch, while they're up, up there looking for you?'

'Yup,' he agreed.

'But . . . but Grumpy and some of the hands are still there.'

He frowned. 'Yeah. I didn't count on that. That's why we was just sorta layin' back, figurin' out what to do. But then you rode up here, so we didn't have to figure out a way to get you away from the place. I bet you just did that so I'd find you, didn't you?'

'No!' she said, much louder than she intended.

He grinned. 'Aw, I bet you did. I bet you was just sittin' here wishin' I'd show up like one o' them knights, to rescue you an' ride off with you. So that's just what I come to do.'

'What? Are you out of your mind? I don't have any intention of going anywhere with you.'

'Aw, of course you do. Besides, you ain't got a whole lotta choice.'

'What do you mean?'

He shrugged. 'I mean, when I decide a woman oughta do somethin', she just naturally does it, that's all. Part of bein' a man, you know. A real man. I bet you don't know what it's like to have a real man, do you? That's all right. You'll learn right shortly. Not right now, though. I gotta admit, I'd love to take you right here, with Wes standin' over there watchin', but that ain't a good idea. We'd best get some distance behind us, just in case that posse wises up an' comes lookin' for you.'

As he talked, her face became increasingly red, more with anger than embarrassment. She swung at him as hard as she could. He laughed, catching her hand in mid-swing. His grip felt like a steel vise clamped onto her wrist.

'Well now, that ain't polite,' he chided her, 'tryin' to slap me just for lettin' you know how smitten I am with you. That's all right. You'll be a whole lot tamer afore daylight, I promise you. Now come on and get on your horse. We gotta ride.'

She jerked and struggled against him. 'I will do no such thing! Let loose! You're hurting my wrist.'

Ignoring her protests, he began to walk toward the horses, dragging her along. She pulled back, tried to plant her feet, tried to jerk from his grasp, all to no avail. He moved her toward the horses as inexorably as a moth toward a candle. A feeling of helpless despair swept suddenly over her, and she struggled to keep from folding up on the ground.

He jerked her roughly. 'Now don't go

pullin' nothin' like that. Get on your horse.'

Her mind cast about frantically. She looked into his eyes, and saw only an icy glint that made her shudder. Numbly she put a foot in the stirrups and swung into the saddle.

He whipped a pigging string from his back pocket and slipped a loop of it over one of her wrists. 'Sorry about this, sweetheart,' he smiled. 'I just can't take a chance on your tryin' something that'd slow us down. We gotta put some miles behind us, so we can afford the time to find us a real fine place to camp for the night.'

As he secured her wrists tightly to the saddle horn, he lowered his voice. 'Tell you what, though. You cooperate, and I'll fix you'n me a bed away from where Wes can hear us or see us. Besides, you'll enjoy the night a whole lot more thataway. Funny about that. Whether it's the worst night of your life or the best night of your life just depends on how you approach it. I'll enjoy it more if you're likin' it too.'

At a complete loss for words, she sputtered helplessly. Grinning, he stepped into his own saddle. Holding the reins of her horse in his hand, he nudged his horse into a swift trot. Wes fell in line behind her, and they rode, heading south and east.

17

The horse's breathing became more labored by the mile. Fuming inside, Lonnie forced himself to let the animal slow from a lope to a fast trot. The country went by agonizingly slowly. He lashed himself mentally for being so slow-witted. He tried to force himself not to think of Corky with Arn.

He was not very successful. Images of the cocky gunman having Corky at his mercy kept popping into his mind.

Convincing himself the horse's breathing had slowed, he spurred him back into a lope. He rode over the last rise on his approach to the ranch. He stood in the stirrups. His eyes pried into every nook and cranny of the yard, looking for something amiss.

Grumpy Wollesen was limping across the yard, a bucket of oats in his hand. He stopped and looked up at the sound of Lonnie's approach.

Another hand, working with a colt in the round corral, appeared not to notice him at all. They were the only two people visible as he rode in.

'Tryin' to kill that horse?' Grumpy called.

'Where's Corky?' Lonnie demanded, ignoring the flunkee's comment.

Grumpy frowned. 'Ain't my day to keep track of her,' he groused. 'I got enough stuff to keep track of around here without tryin' to keep track of her too.'

'Is she here?' Lonnie demanded.

His grousing cowed by Lonnie's intensity, the old man shook his head. 'Nope. She rode out.'

'Where'd she go?'

Grumpy's truculence returned. 'That's somethin' I'm supposed to know? I'm a flunkee, 'cause I'm too old an' busted-down to be a cowpoke. That don't make me nursemaid to the boss's kid. She's a big girl. Saddles her own horses. Gets on all by herself. Reins 'em where she wants to go. She don't ask me where she kin ride to, an' I don't try to tell 'er.'

Resisting the urge to ride up and kick the old man in the face, Lonnie gritted, 'Arn and Wes are after her. I got to know where she is!'

Awareness dawned on the old man, changing his expression completely. He swore. 'Sorry. I didn't know that. I don't got no idee where she went. Her ma prob'ly does. Want me to holler at what boys is left here?'

Lonnie stepped from the saddle. 'No. Just saddle me a different horse, would you?'

'I kin do that. What horse you want?'

'The big Arabian here?'

Grumpy nodded. 'He's in the barn.'

'Saddle him. He can run forever.'

Without a word Grumpy took the reins from his hand and limped toward the barn. Lonnie sprinted to the house.

Theda heard his boots clumping on the porch and started to rise. She gasped in surprise as he burst in the door.

'Ma'am, where'd Corky go?'

Her eyes wide in astonishment, Theda said, 'She rode up to the rim, Lonnie. Why?'

Lonnie swore. 'I think Arn and Wes set the whole thing up just to get everyone away from the ranch. I think Arn's after Corky.'

Theda gasped. Her hands flew to her mouth. Her eyes stared in horror.

'Oh! She was so worried about you that she couldn't stand to sit around and wait any longer. I finally let her go for a ride. I'm sure that's where she went. Oh, Lonnie, don't let him have my girl!'

'I'll find 'em,' Lonnie promised as he whirled to go.

'Wait!' Theda called. 'You need to take somebody with you.'

'Ain't got time,' he called over his shoulder.

Grumpy was just limping out of the barn. He led a dark sorrel Arabian stallion that stood fully sixteen hands high. Muscles rippled with every step.

Grumpy said, 'At least he's in good shape. Ira's been runnin' 'im twice a week all summer. Says he's keepin' him healthy, but I think he just likes the feel o' him runnin'. Don't you go puttin' a foot in a prairie-dog hole or somethin', now. You kill this horse the boss'll never let you have Corky.'

Ignoring the old man's constant chatter, Lonnie sprang into the saddle. He jabbed his spurs into the stud's sides much harder than he intended. The stallion snorted and leaped forward. By the end of the yard he was running flat out. His belly seemed almost to touch the top of the grass.

Lonnie grinned in spite of the tenseness of the situation. The world around him turned to a blur. Wind rushed past his ears. He pulled his hat down tightly. As soon as he let loose of it, the brim blew up flat against the crown. It felt as if a hand were pushing against his forehead, trying to push him back out of the saddle.

He let the horse run flat out for two miles, then hauled on the reins to urge him to a more reasonable pace. The great stallion shook his head, fighting the bit. Lonnie shrugged. 'Well, if you ain't ready to slow down, have at it, big boy!'

The country sped past. He passed the meadow where he had picked a bouquet of wild flowers for Corky the year before. He had handed them to her, hoping they would convey the depths of his feelings for her. She admired the flowers, but said nothing of him, frustrating him, leaving him helpless before the intensity of his love.

He raced through the valley where her horse had run away, that same summer. He had raced after them and caught it, roping it before it could fall or hurt her. She had tumbled out of the saddle into his arms, and he had held her until she stopped trembling. His heart tried hard to convince him that she stayed in his arms a lot longer than her fear required, but he was afraid to pursue it. He wondered suddenly if her horse had actually been running away, or if she had engineered the whole thing.

He passed the rocks where they had sat eating a picnic lunch. He couldn't remember the reason she had requested that he accompany her. He remembered only the day they spent together, chattering and playing like a couple school children. It had been one of the happiest days of his life.

His horse leaped across the stream of clear mountain water without slowing in the least. He remembered that creek. Half a mile downstream there was a wide, clear pool. One summer day a year ago they had sat together. Jokingly he had invited her to go swimming with him. She had slapped him so hard his head rang, gotten on her horse, and rode back to the ranch alone. It was several days before he realized he had been talking, a few minutes before, of skinny-dipping in the creek as a boy. He had teased her about it later, asking her why she thought about skinny-dipping when he hadn't even thought of it.

Thompson Rim loomed in the distance. He stood in the stirrups, straining his eyes for any glimpse of the Appaloosa gelding.

Suddenly he caught sight of movement. He reined the stallion in, ignoring his insistence that he be allowed to run.

Fully two miles away, to his left, moving south and east, three dots moved in a line. With the vision of one accustomed to great distances and the clear air of the mountains, he studied them.

'That's them,' he gritted. 'They got 'er already. She's in the saddle, though.'

He lifted the horse's reins, noting with amazement that the great stallion was scarcely breathing hard. He had run flat out for nearly ten miles, and wanted to run some more.

'Go get 'em, boy,' he said, touching the horse with his spurs.

The horse responded instantly, nearly jumping out from under Lonnie. In half a dozen strides he was running flat out again. He appeared to spot the object of their search almost immediately, and bore a course directly toward them.

'Got 'em spotted, too, ain't you,' Lonnie gritted.

His quarry neared visibly. They became distinguishable as horses and riders, rather than just dots. Fifteen minutes later, he could begin to pick out features of the three.

'Got her in the middle,' he observed.

Another fifteen minutes later he was less than half a mile behind them, closing fast.

It was shortly after that that their horses, or one of them, heard his approach. He saw Arn whirl to look over his shoulder, then jerk erect. Too far away to hear, he saw him say something. The other two whirled to look his direction as well. Then Arn turned his horse and moved in front of Corky. Wes reined his horse around and took up a position to Arn's left, twenty feet or so away from him.

Lonnie hauled on the reins of the great stallion, fighting him, forcing him to slow. He slowed at last, his front legs slamming jarringly as he came to a stop. He continued to prance and toss his head, pleading for freedom to run again. Lonnie knew the great animal would run until he collapsed and died if he allowed him to, or asked him to. Now his prancing and fidgeting made it impossible to hope to shoot straight from his back.

He nudged the horse forward, prancing and dancing until he was fifty feet from the pair of outlaws.

Arn grinned. 'Well, now. Ain't this just too good to be true!'

Lonnie stepped from the saddle. He stood still for a moment, to allow his legs to adjust to the change. Then he stepped away from the stallion. He dropped the reins, aware with some portion of his mind of the animal continuing to toss his head and stomp his feet, but bound by training to stay where he was as long as the reins remained on the ground.

His eyes darted to Corky. He noted the cord binding her wrists to the saddle horn. A sense of relief flooded over him, leaving him almost weak. Some part of his mind he dared not probe had feared she was riding with them of her own free will, and he didn't think he could have endured that. Now he knew she was a prisoner, and something within him wanted to shout with joy.

As his hand brushed the butt of his gun, Arn spoke again. 'Sometimes a plan works so good it seems almost impossible,' he exulted. 'Here I am, ridin' outa the country with the woman I been havin' all them dreams about, just so I can make all them dreams real. The only thing that's bothered me about a perfect plan to do that, is leavin' one piece o' unfinished business behind. I was leavin' without a chance to get even for a whippin' I took. I'da killed you right where you stood that day, if Bull hadn't been there protectin' Pretty Boy with that shotgun. And then, just when I'm leavin' the country, here comes Pretty Boy, ridin' hell-for-leather, just to give me a chance to do that.'

As he talked, Lonnie felt a sinking sensation in his gut. The whole time he had ridden after them, his only thought had been for Corky. He had given no thought to what he would do when he found them.

Now he stood there, facing Arn and Wes together. Both men were relaxed, confident. They had good right to be. On his very best day, Lonnie knew he didn't have a ghost of a chance against Arn. Wes was a different matter. Lonnie was no slouch with a gun. He was confident he could handle the lesser man. But Arn was a gunman with a skill unmatched by anyone Lonnie had ever heard of.

He knew with a cold certainty that as soon as he touched his gun he would be dead. He knew that Corky was going to watch him die. Then Arn and Wes would ride off with her, unmoved by her grief. Arn would do whatever he wanted to with her, for as long as he wanted to. Then he would give her to Wes. The woman he loved was about to be turned over to a fate worse than death, and there was nothing he could do to stop it.

His mind cast about desperately for some way out of the situation. Why hadn't he thought this through earlier? Why hadn't he ridden to some point ahead of them, and lain in ambush. If he had hidden, shot Arn from ambush, then he could have saved her. Now, instead, he had condemned himself to death and Corky to much worse.

He swallowed, trying hard to slow the frantic thrashing of his mind. His eyes darted to Corky, then back to Arn. Even in that instant he saw the fear and despair in her eyes. He knew she understood the situation as clearly as he.

'There ain't no way you can get away with this,' he bluffed. 'The whole country'll come lookin' for you. You can't ride far enough to get away, if you do this. Ride off and leave her here, and I'll let you ride away.'

Arn chuckled. 'Listen to yourself, Pretty Boy,' he said. 'It'd make more sense for you to beg. In fact, you beg a little, and I'll let you live long enough to come along and watch me tame this woman you thought was gonna be yours, how's that sound.'

As Arn talked, Lonnie saw Corky using her legs to turn her horse. He figured out instantly that she was trying to get her horse turned in such a way that she could jam her spurs into his sides, sending him careening into Arn's horse. If she could succeed, he might just have a chance.

Just as hope surged in him, her horse moved a couple steps and stepped on the reins Arn had dropped on the ground. It stopped instantly. No amount of nudging by her knees could induce the horse to turn further. If she spurred him turned the way he was, he would only run away, and that distraction would not be nearly enough.

Despair filled the place in the center of his being where hope had almost blossomed. There was absolutely no way out of his dilemma.

'Well, Pretty Boy, you gonna go for that gun, or do I get to just shoot you like a dog?' Arn taunted.

High in the sky, Lonnie caught a glimpse of movement. Trying to look without moving his eyes, he finally realized what it was. A great bald eagle had folded its wings and was plummeting earthward in a blur of speed. Despair returned with the realization that an eagle was simply hunting, and had spotted some prey that was about to become its dinner.

Then, with a start, he realized what the prey was. The tail of the squirrel the eagle hated so much trailed from the back of Arn's hatband. The eagle had spotted it, and interpreted it as the squirrel, perched on top of the man's head.

He had no more time to think. The streaking eagle opened its great wings just as its talons touched the hat. Its whole weight slammed into the top and back of Arn's head with the force of a sledge-hammer. He flew from the saddle, sprawled face down, unmoving on the ground. Blood poured from deep gouges in his scalp.

The eagle lifted with the beating of its giant wings. Firmly gripped in its talons, Arn's hat dangled, with its trophy fluttering softly in the breeze.

The three watched with open-mouthed amazement as the eagle mounted the air in a spiral, winging its way higher and higher until it was a dot in the distant sky. From there it dropped the hat, that it undoubtedly still thought was a squirrel, to be smashed to oblivion on the rocks a mile below.

The instant it dropped the hat, Lonnie's attention snapped back to

Wes. He walked several steps toward him. 'Well, Wes? What's it to be? Throw up your hands, and I'll take you to town to stand trial. Otherwise go for your gun.'

Wes swallowed visibly. His eyes darted up to the hat, fluttering earthward. They jerked to Arn, lying motionless on the ground. They whipped back to Lonnie. He swallowed hard again. Then he abruptly grabbed for his gun.

Lonnie's draw was smooth and swift. He was right. Though no match for Arn, he was no slouch with a gun. His gun leaped into his hand, spouting fire and lead at the hapless follower Arn had towed around in his wake. He died as he had lived, in foolish futility. He toppled from the saddle, dead before he touched the ground. His gun landed harmlessly on the ground beside him.

Lonnie sighed, and holstered his gun. He hurried to Corky, drawing his knife as he walked. Neither spoke as he sliced through the pigging string that had bound her to her saddle. She toppled out of that saddle into his arms.

He held her tightly against himself, as her arms wrapped around him. They stood there, her face buried against his chest, for several minutes. Slowly, he felt the tension leave her body. She moved back slightly, tipping her face up toward him.

It seemed like an invitation to him. One he surely had no intention of turning down. He kissed her slowly, then feverishly, raining kisses on her face, her hair, her neck. She returned them all, as best she was able.

'Oh, darling,' she said, 'I was so afraid. I knew Arn would kill you, and then I'd have nobody, and he'd do all the things he said he was going to do, and I couldn't stop him. And then that eagle came. Oh, Lonnie, the eagle killed him. I never saw anything like that!'

They were interrupted by a harsh voice. 'Not quite.'

They both whirled as if they had

been struck. Arn stood, spraddle-legged. Blood covered his shoulders and dripped from his hair.

'Just took my hat,' he bragged. 'Thought he'd killed me, huh? Takes a lot more than that to kill Arnett Banning. Takes a whole lot more than you, too, Pretty Boy. Now I'm gonna kill you. Then I'm gonna let that woman o' yours lick all this blood off of me. Then I'm gonna teach her what a real man's like. I'm tired o' waitin', Pretty Boy. Go for your gun!'

Lonnie stepped away from Corky. The sickeningly familiar feeling of despair filled his stomach. Wounded as he was, he knew with absolute certainty that Arn could kill him easily.

With no choices left, Lonnie jerked his gun from its holster. As though watching his own death in slow motion, he watched Arn's gun clear the holster and lift toward him. His own gun was just clearing the holster as Arn's gun came into alignment with his chest.

In that same slow motion, he saw a

large hole appear in the center of Arn's chest. He saw the gunman jerk backward. He saw fire blossom from the end of Arn's gun barrel. He felt the angry buzz of a bullet pass his ear. Only then did he hear the booming roar of a Sharps fifty from somewhere behind him.

Arn toppled backward, sprawled on the ground. His right arm extended at right-angles to his body. His gun was still in his hand. His eyes were open, staring sightlessly into the blue sky.

Lonnie whirled, searching the edge of the timber behind him. Montana Keep stepped into view, a Sharps long rifle hanging easily from his hand. He waved, as if greeting a friend at a barn dance.

Lonnie started to wave. A strange choking sound caught his attention. Then he realized it was coming from his own mouth. He swallowed. He turned to Corky. She flew into his arms, sobbing with relief and joy.

They pried themselves from each

other a moment later. They turned to face Montana. His crooked brown teeth grinned at them.

'You two all right?' the mountain man asked.

Lonnie swallowed again. 'We are now,' he said. 'Where'd you come from?'

Montana chuckled. 'I spotted them two sneakin' outa thet box canyon yesterday. Thought I oughta see what they was up to. Me'n Billy Boy been shadowin' 'em. I was fixin' to spring a little surprise on 'em, when I seed you a comin' like a streak. Thought I'd jist sorta bide my time an' see whether I was needed.'

'You was needed!' Lonnie heard himself gush. 'I've never been so glad to see anyone in my life!'

'Me either,' Corky agreed. 'Oh, Montana, I could just kiss you.'

'Well, I cain't say I'd mind that none.' Montana grinned.

So she did. On his grizzled and greasy cheek. But she saved the real kisses for Lonnie. Later.

The stage robbery had been accomplished by an old woman. Twine Fourch had never heard of a female being a highway robber before. He followed the trail all the way to a dilapidated log cabin up Stone Mountain. What happened after that no one could believe even after townsmen from Jefferson found the old log house and the skeletal dying old woman. But before the mystery could be solved there would be two unnecessary killings, a bizarre suicide and a lynching.

GUNS OF THE GAMBLER

M. Duggan

Destitute gambler Ben Crow arrives in Mallory keen to claim his inheritance, only to discover that rancher Edward Bacon has other ideas. Set up by Miss Dorothy, who had fooled him completely, Ben finds himself dangling on the end of a rope. Saved from death, Ben sets off in pursuit of Miss Dorothy, determined upon retribution. However, his quest for vengeance turns into a rescue mission when she is kidnapped by a crazy man-burning bandit.

SIDEWINDER

John Dyson

All Flynn wants is to be Marshal of Tucson, but he is framed by the territory's richest rancher, Frank Buchanan, and thrown into Yuma prison. Five years later Flynn comes out, intent on clearing his name and burning for vengeance. Fists thud, knives flash and bullets fly as he rides both sides of the law and participates in kidnapping and double-dealing. He is once again arrested for a murder of which he is innocent. Can he escape the noose a second time?

THE BLOODING OF JETHRO

Frank Fields

When Jethro Smith's family is murdered by outlaws, vengeance is the one thing on his mind. He meets the brother of one of the murderers, who attempts to exploit Jethro's grudge in the pursuit of his own vendetta. The local preacher, formerly a sheriff, teaches Jethro how to use a gun. With his new-found skills, Jethro and his somewhat unwelcome friend pit themselves against seemingly impossible odds. Whatever the outcome lead would surely fly.